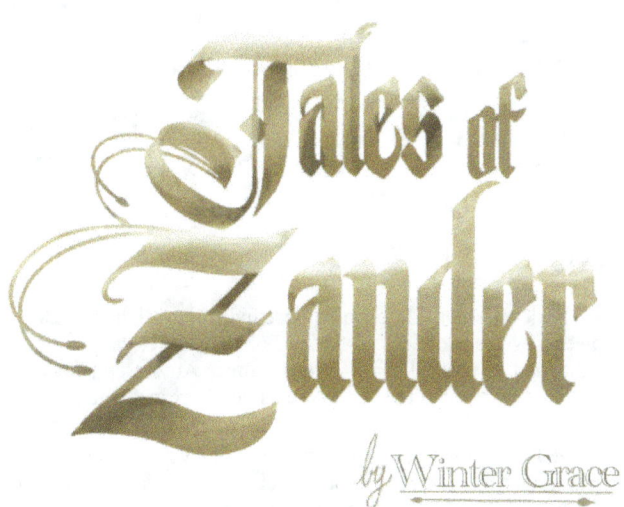

Tales of Zander

by Winter Grace

First Printing: 2024
Alanna Rusnak Publishing

Library and Archives Canada Cataloguing in Publication
CIP data on file with the National Library and Archives

ISBN trade paperback edition: 978-1-990336-75-1

Illustrations by M. Adelle Laporte

Alanna Rusnak Publishing is an imprint of Chicken House Press

282906 Normanby/Bentinck Townline
Durham, Ontario, Canada, N0G 1R0
www.chickenhousepress.ca

This book is dedicated to Elise Laporte. Surprise!
Yes, this tome is for you. Thank you for your undying enthusiasm,
your many hugs, and always being there for me. Love you, Elise!

Table of Contents

TALES OF ZANDER

Winter Grace

The Forbidden Swamp

Year 463 of the Second Millenia

The Forbidden Swamp

Long, long ago, when the province of Jarrel was a nameless wasteland and Warrick a tangled swamp, a delicate girl was born by the fire's glow. Her parents named her Zemira so that her life might be a song for all to hear. That girl was me, and though I am not fond of the term delicate, it suited me all too well.

Born two months before my time, I nearly died that same day. However, the Master had other plans for me. Important ones it seemed. Although I did not know them for years to come.

I was *not* malformed, merely small. The visitors who claimed such were wrong in every estimation. My growth, while somewhat stunted, was steady. Healthy even. Alas, my size mattered more to others than it should have. In short, it bothered them. In long, they felt they needed to overcompensate by babying me.

"I'm still growing," I always reminded them. My worried elders nodded and smiled every time. They pandered me. They catered to my childish independence for fear of upsetting that delicate balance that was my strength.

I am four feet and three inches. I am not that short! I often yearned to say. I knew better than to try. Informing other pre-adolescent girls of this fact proved even more futile than reasoning with the adults. Eventually, I gave up...

* * *

My thirteenth birthday dawned rich and pure. Sunbeams shot through sheer curtains and dust motes to dazzle my groggy eyes. I hauled myself out of my bedsheets. The sickly-sweet warmth of prolonged sleep fled my body. Humid air assaulted my bare arms. Sweat glistened upon my ebony skin, as shiny and slick as it was disgusting. Shivering in abhorrence, I scrambled into a simple dress and allowed my feet to remain unshod. The smooth floor creaked lightly beneath my toes.

I tiptoed halfway down the lofty staircase, silent as the stars.

"You can't protect her forever. She is going to find out eventually."

I froze mid step. *Momma? What in Zander is she talking about?* My ears strained as I waited for Pappa to respond. Bad of me, I know, but I could never help myself with such things. It was either walk away or eavesdrop. I chose the latter.

An exasperated sigh split the air.

"The world has no need for another Defendant. Zander is safe for the time being. Warrick especially. What would she even represent? Zemira is still too young. The other defenders were much older when they discovered their destinies. She will be the same."

"Runa said she would be the next guardian. You cannot stop fate."

Runa? Defender of Knowledge? I waited with bated breath. My tiny fingers clutched the railing until my knuckles shone pale through the skin. Legend said Runa hadn't been seen in fifty years! Not since Jarrel joined the Defendants and ended the Severing War. Or so the legends claimed. When had my parents spoken with her?

*Maybe I should go back…*I thought with reluctance. Their conversation was obviously private. Perhaps if I managed to sneak back under my covers I could—

"Zemira?" Pappa's voice ended my delusions. I could no longer return from whence I came. Calm and curious, I descended the remainder of the stairwell. My parents glanced toward one another in that wordless adult language of theirs. Unfortunately for them, I understood every unspoken syllable.

"Are you going to tell her, or shall I?"

"Should we tell her at all?"

"This is a horrible idea."

I nearly rolled my eyes.

"What are you hiding from me?" I asked plainly. Understandable as it was, glances and gestures paled in comparison to direct conversation. My parents shifted, visibly agitated. I waited, silently demanding their answers.

Momma sighed and ran her fingers through her tight curls.

"I don't know what to tell you, Zemira. Would you mind stepping outside while Pappa and I finish our discussion?"

I bit my lips to restrain a sigh. Nevertheless, I obeyed. Methodical as always, I stepped into my overlarge galoshes. I walked slowly. Perhaps, if I took long enough, they would change their minds.

They did not. Both watched me with a silent patience that could rival geodes growing within their stones. The door clicked sharply behind me as I left, letting the latch fall into place. Stagnant air stuck to my lungs while I drew a long, steadying breath. The waterlogged porch squelched beneath my leather galoshes. Rancid air bubbled up through the swampy underbrush below.

Noxious gasses wafted from the dead waters. Marsh wove between bent willow and sagging beech. Moss devoured. Toxins destroyed. All the while I stood helpless upon my raised porch.

I had called my homeland many things throughout my life. Pleasant was not one of them.

My eyes trailed the dying realm I called my own, mapping out an invisible pathway. Mossy stones and rotten logs stretched from one landmass to the next in a perfect Zemira-sized route. I imagined myself venturing into the wild swamplands. Alone. No one to bother me or call me insignificant. Just me, the Master of All Worlds, and the frogs.

The slimy peepers croaked nearby, always eager to snatch midges from the air with their lengthy tongues. I smiled at one and stuck out my tongue to match. My green companion plopped into the murky waters in reply.

I sighed, swinging my legs over the edge of the porch. My covered toes brushed the damp ground. Sludgy water coated the leather of my boots. One step, one misguided footfall, and I would be lost to the poisonous mire.

Muffled voices tickled my ears from behind the latched door. Tantalizing, secretive voices that lured me closer. My ears twitched. Their pointed helixes flicked the side of my head. Eavesdropping seemed inevitable. Unless…

"Unless I take a walk."

Without thought, hesitation, or plan, I kicked off my galoshes and leapt into the swamp.

My bare feet sunk several inches into the quagmire. The miasmal gasses bubbled and hissed beneath my toes. The ground felt alive. It breathed. Sickly, heaving breaths stirred the muck in shuddering eddies. I drew a shallow draught of air, the bitter aether somehow sweet as I stepped further into the unknown.

Within minutes, I learned the true joy of a coddiwomple. To travel purposefully in whatever vague direction I pleased, relishing in my adventure. Not that I was running away or anything drastic. Just a simple jaunt in the swamp, see? A walk.

I passed my family's sunken property marker without a thought, venturing into wilds I had yet to explore.

One foot after the other. One step and then another. Tiptoed tread morphed into capers and bounds. I danced from log to stone, wary of possible monsters yet ever so carefree. Moss oozed underfoot. Rotten wood crumbled as I scampered across long-dead trees sunk in their watery graves. Bulrushes tickled my arms and nose. Some towered high above my head, giants to my diminutive self. Fungus coiled up gnarled tree trunks. The iridescent mushrooms sprouted from arbor and ground alike, glowing an insipid blackish green.

It could be beautiful. If it were not so sickly, I would say it already is, I thought to myself. But the drooping foliage made the swamp's state perfectly clear: Warrick was dying. How long until its people followed suit?

I wandered deeper into the marshy wood. The sun rose high in his heavenly belfry. Stunning rays coaxed life into the despondent plants, lifting their weary heads skyward. I did the same. Closing my eyes, I hopped onto a rock and lifted my face to catch the sunbeams.

My stomach grumbled loud enough to scare the passing toads. Only then did I realize it was noon.

Noon!

I jolted, nearly stumbling from my perch. I had left in the early morning! Before breakfast even. Judging by the sudden aching of my stomach, it was high time for lunch as well. I glanced behind me in a panic. The path I took laid in a haphazard line of debris and terrain. Half sunken footholds marked where I *might* have once stood. I gazed frantically about but couldn't tell where exactly I came from.

"Oh dear…" I whispered. The trees, once sickly to my sympathetic eyes, became menacing. Hostile eyes gleamed from every shadow. Frogs peeped. Gasses hissed. Grass rustled and creaked in a stifling breeze. I trembled, unsure of whence I came or where to go.

"Dear oh dear oh dear oh dear." It was all I could

manage to say as the panic fluttered in my chest. I whirled about, searching for any trace or footprint that might betray my path homeward. It was too late. The muck had already swallowed my trail.

Growls rose from the underbrush and cascaded from the treetops. Eerie eyes peeked through the foliage. Owl eyes in a feathered, draconic face peered from below. A dracal. A series of slitted, golden eyes leered from above. Goblins.

Nope! No monsters for me today, thanks. I fled.

I gave up on direction altogether and ran. Bushes swished and susurrated, whispering amongst themselves as my parents had done. Crows and ravens shrieked overhead. Frogs chirruped. Midges whined. I whimpered, pressing my hands securely over my ears. Fear quickened my breath and lent wings to my feet. Heedless of my surroundings, I plunged deeper into the swamp.

The ground shifted beneath my frantic footfalls. Water gurgled and frothed through the moss. Gnarled trees snagged my arms and face. Their timber claws raked across my dress, tearing fringe and bodice alike. I stumbled onward, terrified.

Something rigid caught my foot. I screamed, tumbling headlong onto solid ground.

Solid?

Slimy foliage ensnared my arms and stuck in my open mouth. I sputtered and gagged. Apparently, the rotten undergrowth tasted as awful as it smelled.

I wiped the grime from my eyes. The sludge stung wherever it touched, temporarily blinding me. The poisonous flora left an acrid taste upon my tongue even as I scraped it away. I stood, brushing bits of bulrush from my grazed knees. Black and white splotches danced across my vision as I puzzled through the fogbank that encompassed my mind.

"Where...am I?" My fright evaporated. Curiosity replaced it in a twinkling. I tested the ground, stomping repeatedly on the hard-packed turf. Solid. Far sturdier than my porch had ever been. Yellowed grass sprouted from the suspiciously firm ground in tufts.

I paced the island's perimeter. Muddy tracks marked the beginning, end, and median of my trail. I planted my hands on my hips, surveying my footprints upon the grass.

"A perfect circle..." I mused. The circular islet rose upward from where I stood. The steady incline escalated inward for a good hundred metres before it dipped into itself. Strain as I might, I could not see within the divot from my vantage point. Only one solution remained.

Huffing, I strode up the hillock. Dead grass crunched underfoot. Deranged birds cawed and cackled overhead like a gaggle of witches. The ever-stagnant air cloyed my lungs. I coughed it away, pressing forward.

I reached the summit in a matter of moments. The land dipped sharply. My toes hung over the ridge, curled upon the lower edge. Craning my neck, I gazed down into a paradise.

A swamp to be specific. Only the swampland in the island's core was not miasmal or dead. It was healthy, warm, and full of life. Verdant mosses hugged log, and stone, and soil. Shrubs spurted from the heath in cheerful clumps. A dusky pool wavered about an even smaller island at the valley bottom. Waterlilies rimmed the basin in the approximation of a circle. Something rusted and perfectly straight jutted from the island's centre.

I slid down the gully. Slime lubricated my feet, easing my travel immensely. Pebbles crunched as the lush verdure flattened underfoot. I skittered to a halt, inches from the pole.

No, not a pole. A spear.

A gentle wind stirred in the dell. Rust flaked off the spear haft. Metal gleamed beneath the crimson coat. Overcome by wonder, I stretched out my hand. My fingers inched toward the weapon, eager yet hesitant.

"Help me…" something pleaded, the voice sinking into the mire. Only it was not a voice. If anything, it was a consciousness.

Pain washed over me. A despair of body and soul that did not originally belong within my heart. It belonged to Warrick. I gasped, spasming as the swamp itself called for aid. My soul ached for the dying land, filled with an all-consuming hunger for rebirth.

Something rose from my skin, ephemeral and warm. Embers. Well, the *appearance* of embers. Each one wavered about me, connected as they were distant. They spread outward to the farthest reaches of the swamp. As the embers settled into the miasmal muck, comfort wafted through the land. The comfort of a warm hearth and loving family. Of Healing.

"Free me," the wan voice begged. Whether nymph, sprite, or spirit, the swamp was desperate. *He* was desperate. My eyes drifted to the rusted spear rammed into Warrick's heart. *"Please…free me…"*

Without thinking, I gripped the spear in both hands and *pulled*.

Lightning flashed. The spear burst alight with all the warmth and comfort of glowing embers. Rust fell away in a shower of amber light. Water stirred as the ground rumbled. Waves sloshed up to my knees, responding to the sudden disruption. I staggered away from the riled pool. Shrieking, I tossed the spear aside. Only…the spear didn't budge. The metallic haft cleaved to my right hand, bound by its amber glow.

Orange phosphorescence glimmered where the spear once stood. It rose high into the air. A pillar of light. A beacon to all the weary souls lost within the Warrick swamplands. I gazed up at it, gripping the rust-free pole for support.

Amber waves pulsed from the beacon. A deliciously cold gale tumbled up from the pond, washing over me. The most pleasant of scents chased away the stench of death. Fresh air. Never did I know such an aroma existed. It was a smell I swore neither to forget nor take for granted.

With the spear stuck fast to my hand, I ascended the gully. I froze midway up the slope. My stunned eyes roved over the scenery as amber light throbbed overhead. I gazed in wonder at my homeland. Healthful swamps stretched endlessly unto the horizon.

My home was cured.

Some ambiguous force bound death to life across the waters. Plants still decayed. Midges and frogs continued to swarm. Yet the land was renewed. No one who saw it would dare say otherwise.

The beacon vanished in a blaze of persimmon and embers. Starlike fragments rained around me. Some morphed into gentle flames. Others diffused midair. The lights that remained trailed deep into the marsh. A winding path shone beneath their kindly glow. One flitted o'er the solid islet. It paused a handbreadth away from my face.

"Hello?" I offered. In reply, the orange flare streaked downward and seeped into my chest.

I gasped. A warm thrill entered my heart. Oddly enough, the warmth felt *right*. Like a fire in the hearth or laughter in a home. Somehow, it belonged to me and I to it.

Defender, my mind whispered. My poor parents. By sending me outside, they brought into being the very thing they feared: my destiny. A fate beyond my imagination awaited. Somewhere down that endless trail of flamelike wisps, destiny called.

I bounded down the island hill. Where yellowed grass once grew, vibrant green replaced it. I leapt onto a moss-cloaked rock, giggling. The natural carpet squished beneath my toes. Water black as midnight and twice as deep lurked beyond my perch. Ebony waves teemed with fish, salamanders, and the omnipresent frogs.

The spear, though crafted of metal, did not hinder me. It was neither cumbersome nor hollow. Some mystic metal forged shaft and spearhead, blending them seamlessly into one. Strange as it was, the slender lance fit my palm to perfection. I could only conclude that it was made for me to find and keep. How else could I carry a five-foot metal pole? I was tiny!

I hopped, skittered, and stumbled along the wisp-lit path. Each leading lantern soaked into my chest as I passed. Familiar swamplands sped by underfoot, but I ignored them. I drank in their newfound beauty whilst disregarding their geography. It wasn't until an elevated cabin appeared through the knobby trees that I realized where I stood.

"Home!" I cried out joyfully. The flickering wisps had led me home. They vanished upon my exclamation, for their job was done. I no longer needed them as guides. My feet found well-known footholds in the shifting landscape. I streaked across them in a heartbeat.

I hauled myself onto the still-slimy deck, stumbling over my galoshes as I ran for the door. Yanking it open, I shouted, "Momma! Pappa! I'm so—"

Five strangers lounged about the living room, conversing as Momma served tea. Two men, three women, and my parents. All seven individuals turned to me, expectant.

"Sorry?"

The strangers went silent. My parents glanced to one another for support. For empathy. Always with that infernal eye-language. I must have looked an absolute mess. Dress torn, feet bare, spear aloft, and my whole body coated in slime. I turned to Momma. The redness of her eyes betrayed tears recently shed. Tears that were my fault entirely.

"Who are these people?" my eyes asked with a slow blink. Rather than answer my unspoken question, Momma scooped me into a spine-crushing hug. I wheezed, too surprised to be grateful.

"Zemira, thank the Master you're safe! Where were you? We were terrified. Is that...?"

Momma trailed off. Her doe eyes trained on my spear, somewhere between horrified and curious.

"A spear," I answered. I held the weapon out for her appraisal, offering my most innocent smile alongside it. Perhaps I could win her favour before she had a chance to ground me. A scoff erupted from the guests.

"She can't be," the visitor muttered. He was a brash looking young man with bloodred eyes and cinnamon skin. The man balanced a halberd on his lap, prepared for battle. A pale woman stood smiling at his side. Shuriken and a full quiver of arrows adorned her belt. Her blue feathered wings glowed with pleasure.

"She is," the woman answered.

Pappa stepped forward, taking my free hand in both of his.

"Zemira," he said, bracing himself, "we would like you to meet your new friends. Runa, Jarrel, Althea, Castiel, and Avril."

"New friends?" I turned toward the strangers to examine them more thoroughly. Each bore a unique weapon. All seemed peaceable. Amicable even. No two visitors looked alike. Almost as if they each stemmed from a different province of Zander. Every province except Warrick.

I stood before the pale winged woman, Runa, my opposite in both stature and complexion.

"Runa. Defender of breath, knowledge, and travel. Am I correct?"

"Correct," Runa smiled. She pressed a wingtip against her chest as she dipped her head in a shallow bow. "Welcome, Zemira. Defendant of Warrick. Keeper of flames, comfort, and rebirth."

The brash man from seconds earlier, undoubtedly Jarrel, stood and planted his halberd on the floor. Scars spanned his tawny neck and arms. The sort that drained one's lifeblood in seconds when first inflicted. The man frowned. Death lingered in that challenging scowl, yet I was not afraid. Especially when he took a knee. It was then I dared to smile and ruffle his feathery hair. Avril guffawed at that. The mace at her hip shook alongside her body.

Jarrel shoved my hand aside, growling. He masked a radiant blush behind his anger. It drew my smile even wider.

"Alright, alright. Welcome to the team." He leaned in close, his hand upon my curly head. "Don't ever do that in public again."

"Understood. Do it in private."

Instead of protesting, Jarrel sighed.

"What does me being a Defender entail?" I asked, glancing from my spear to Runa.

"Responsibilities," Runa said.

"Immortality," added Castiel.

"Helping others," Althea murmured, gazing into the depths of her teacup. Aromatic leaves caught her eye amid the dregs. Entrancing little things.

Avril spread her arms wide, as if inviting all the world into her embrace. "Camaraderie," she chirped. Defender of laughter indeed.

"And sacrifice," said Jarrel. His bloodred eyes flashed a warning. Ever the eye-language with adults it seemed. Sympathy, regret, and a plethora of other melancholy emotions flickered in those crimson irises. That single look possessed no translation in any tongue of human, elf, dwarf, or dracal. Even faerie spells could not craft such gentle pain.

"I understand," I answered. Althea, keeper of truth, glanced up from her tea. She nodded to me, as if to acknowledge the authenticity of my words.

"Are you ready to leave?" Avril jumped to her feet. She held her breath and awaited my answer, leather straps creaking about her legs. Castiel stood at her side. I tilted my head, confused.

"Leave? I thought I was Defendant of Warrick."

"We go where we are needed," Jarrel clarified, clearly biting back a sigh. Not at my ignorance. He sighed at my fate. "Currently, you are needed elsewhere. There was a disturbance in Melian a few days ago that demands our attention. Are you ready to accept this task?"

I opened my mouth to reply but my voice stalled. My parents' faces, eager yet hopeless, burned into my peripheral. Their fates hinged on my answer. For thirteen wonderful years they had raised me. They cared for me, loved me, and protected me from our dangerous homeland. But our home was healed. Warrick was cared for. Zander needed me elsewhere. I could be gone for months, perhaps years. Did I truly have the heart to leave them?

"I don't think I am ready, but I will go. The inevitable is here. Although I do not want to, I know I must say goodbye."

Momma's reddened eyes grew softer as the tears rolled down her cheeks. She gripped Pappa's arm and wept. I threw both arms around them, indulging in tears of my own. Their embrace closed around me. The warmest fire could not compare with the comfort of that hug. Simple as it was, it brought about the end of an era. My childhood ended at the ripe age of thirteen. Eternity waited to succeed it.

My old family released me, relinquishing me to the care of a new one. One I hardly even knew. Jarrel laid a hand on my shoulder. Oddly comforting for the defendant of blood and war. Then again, he embodied loyalty. If only a fraction of the legends were true, I would give him my undying fidelity for as long as we existed.

"Come on, Zemira. I'll teach you how to use that spear when we arrive."

His hand slid from my shoulder. I seized it before he could pull away completely. Maybe, just maybe if I held someone's hand, I wouldn't be so afraid.

Surprisingly, Jarrel allowed it. Avril smothered another giggle fit behind her hand. What she found so funny I might never know. Apparently, I had all of eternity to comprehend her omnipresent sense of humour.

Runa stood in the centre of her five companions. She spread her wings wide enough to encompass us all. My parents stood aside, waving sorrowfully. In a flash of aqua light, my new life began.

I haven't aged a day since.

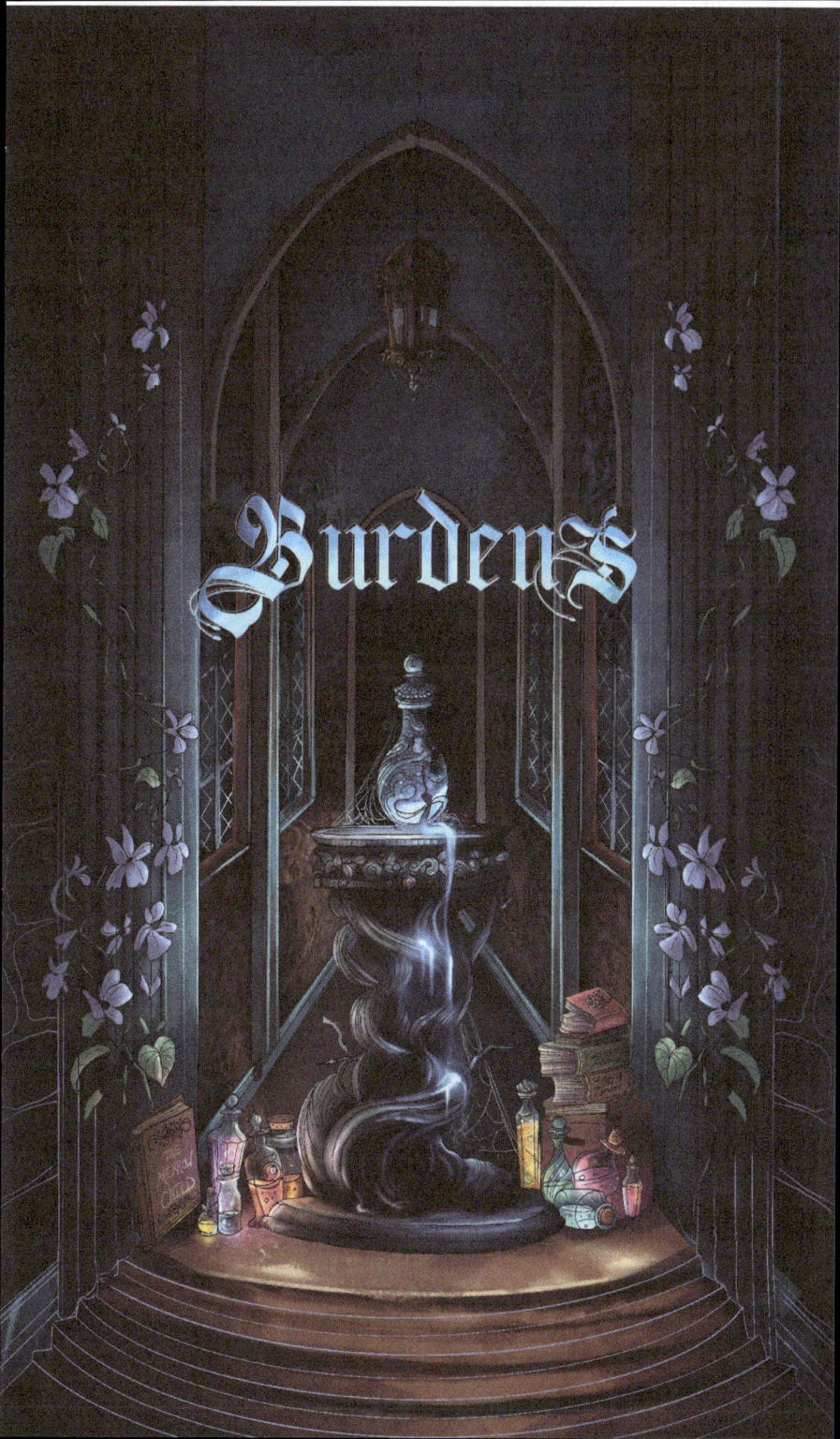

Year 763 of the Second Millenia
— Three Hundred Years Later —

Burdens

Each one of us bears a burden in life. Whether it be one or many, we all have them. Some carry loads more cumbersome than mountains. Others cast off their troubles with ease. Regardless, some burden or other always remains. They are a part of life. An inescapable part. This simple fact can do two things: bind people together or tear them apart.

Imagine a place where all those emotional burdens possessed a physical form. Envision a society cowed by the weight of tangible cares.

Not a pleasant picture, you say? On the contrary, it was incredibly useful. What better way to show a carrier the severity of their burdens than a physical manifestation of each one? A mind of woes is hard to see. A cartload of woes is hard to ignore. Unfortunately, human beings learn to ignore all things with time.

Not so long ago, such a place existed, although its name is nearly forgotten. The inhabitants of this land carried their burdens in glass Vials. More of a tradition than a necessity, although it was infinitely easier than pocketing the emotions. Grief, hatred, and the like filled each bottle accordingly in liquids of vibrant, indistinguishable colours. Colours that merged and shifted with every breath of their carrier, defying all constancy or pattern. One could quite literally pour out their soul to a loved one. It was both marvellous and terrifying.

There were rules to abide by, of course, as with all other nations. For instance, no one could purge their Vials alone. One could not simply dump their troubles in the sea and be done with it. Many tried. All failed. Pilgrimages to hallowed sites, meditation, self-sacrifice. None sufficed. Few solutions ever did. The cursed burdens always returned.

I lived in this land of burdens, and I carried a great many. Grief. Hatred. Self-loathing. Fear. Loss. Sorrow. I carried them all.

"Why do you carry so many? Why are you telling me all this?" you might be thinking. If you are, I like you already. I have my reasons for telling as surely as you have yours for listening. The reason is simple: I am all that is left of Weylin.

Weylin did not end in catastrophe as you might be inclined to think. It did not sink into the sea beneath a crash of mighty waves, nor did it fall to chaos or war. It broke slowly. Deeply. It disintegrated under the weight of burdens left unattended. Vials overflowed. Tensions grew. Eventually, the people of Weylin forsook their homeland. They fled from their burdens, never to be seen again. I alone remained.

Thus, my journey commenced. With Vials brimming and no one to empty them to, I strayed.

Weylin's fall, although no small matter, is not the purpose of this tale. A true tale has no purpose. And so, the story begins.

* * *

I laid alone upon a grassy knoll, the sunrise faint above my head. Stars faded one after another. Clouds rushed by on a gusting spring breeze. Wind roared in its gentle, rustling way as it tore past leaf and reed. Hair tangled about my face. I hardly noticed. My thoughts transcended such meagre annoyances.

My friends. My family. My people. None remained. Every last one of them left, gone to search for whispered freedoms and clearer skies.

Yet the sky above was beautiful to me, clouds and all. Why? I loathed my burdens as much as the next Weylin. Why did they make me stay?

"Someone must remember," I sighed. "Someone must carry on."

Every tragedy claimed a hostage. Every crime had its victim. The captain always sunk with his ship. Only I was not a captain. I was a cabin boy if the crew dared count me at all. Yet someone needed to go down with the ship, and for some reason, everyone turned to me. Whether it was due to my low birth, empathetic Verve, or sheer bad luck I would never know. How could I? I was a mere boy thrust into a world far too wide for my liking.

Beside me, my Vial of resentment burbled and brimmed. I bit back a sigh as the fresh weight settled on my heart. Breathing forcefully, I compressed it. I only owned so many spare Vials. I could not afford for one to overflow or burst.

Nearly a year had passed, yet my peoples' absence still ached, and their abandonment stung. A deathly quietude lingered in the air. Birdsong ceased. Creatures lurked in the woods nearby, unseen and unheeded by their lone human companion.

Lone…

I soon learned what an overstatement that word was.

Bushes crackled as if in a violent gust of wind. Whole branches snapped. I froze, motionless on my grass bed while I listened. Muffled curses punctuated the noise. Strangely enough, the voice uttering said curses was that of a child. Moments later, the culprit burst into the open air amid a torrent of leaves.

He was a scrawny thing, malnourished and unkempt. Age eluded him. Discernable age at least. Young, obviously, but hardened beyond his years. Scraggly hair, worn-out clothing, unshod feet, and eyes wild beyond compare. The frantic boy seemed more beast than human. He spotted me amid the sward and growled.

"Who are you?"

"Weylin," I responded, too shocked for subterfuge.

The wild thing rolled his eyes. "I know *what* you are, wise guy. I'm askin' *who.*"

"Still Weylin."

The boy sneered. "Your parents had a sick sense a' humour."

I laughed. 'Twas a dry, bitter sound that sent both grief and anger bubbling in their casks.

"You don't know the half of it."

"Do too!" the child spat.

I sat up, draping an arm over my raised knee as I met his gaze. He welcomed my motion by skittering several feet away with a snarl. Dogs barked within the forest. The boy shivered. His eyes grew wilder. Panicked breaths heaved behind his visible ribs.

Who hurt you? I thought, standing. The boy flinched. Casually, I collected my Vials and brushed the grass from my legs.

"Do you have a name?" I asked. The boy hesitated, watching with unabashed suspicion as I slung a satchel over my shoulder. Patience was key. If I kept silent, the boy would speak.

"Donovan."

I nodded, expressionless. "Nice to meet you, Donovan, but I should be off. Breakfast won't make itself."

At the mention of breakfast, a rumble disturbed the air. I stifled a smile. Donovan shuffled his bloody feet and clutched his noisome stomach. I made as if to walk away, then paused, glancing back at the half-starved creature.

"Aren't you coming?"

Donovan shrank away. "Why should I?"

"Come on, Donovan. Even the trees can hear your stomach growling. If you want to say no to a decent meal, by all means, say no. My offer stands regardless."

Without another word, I turned homeward. Pale sunlight breached the horizon. It bathed the world in a thousand shades of rose-gold and pink. In that ethereal light, tentative footsteps shuffled alongside me. Laboured breaths mingled with the drowsy animal sounds as the world awoke. Donovan stumbled along, blood and puss oozing from the cuts in his feet.

I can fix that, I told myself. *If he lets me.* Whether he would or not was debatable.

We crossed the field in silence, always keeping left of the wood. Canines howled and yipped in search of a scent. Donovan eyed me, ever tense. Stringy hair obscured his mistrustful gaze. Layers of oil and dust masked the colour of his locks. Filth clung to his skin. Eventually, I gave up deciphering his true appearance. Time would reveal whatever it willed. Lonely as I was, I had all the time in the world. Might as well use it to aid Donovan.

The ground rose steadily. It transitioned from plain, to rise, to incline. Eventually, it grew into a mountain. The steeper the mountain, the slower Donovan walked.

Dogs barked in the near distance, fierce and beastly. The feral sound cascaded down my spine. Shivers wracked my bones. Donovan jolted, whimpering.

My shoulders sagged in relief when a ghost town appeared on the slanted horizon. Smokeless chimneys stabbed the sky above an unwatched wall. Quiet streets wound to and fro. Not a being stirred for there were none. No lamplight shone, only the rising sun. Shop fronts remained shut in disuse. I fingered the key in my pocket with a bitter smile.

Weylin's sole inhabitant had returned.

"Welcome to my city, Donovan. Stay as long as you like."

"Why?" he asked, whispering to pander the silence. "Why are you being nice to me?"

"Companionship?" I offered. Donovan snorted. Whether it was in laughter or derision I could easily guess. Regardless, I led him through the streets to a single-story house near the city's centre. Unlatched shutters swayed on oiled hinges. Loose flagstones composed a ramshackle walkway. Patched curtains drifted through the open windows like vengeful ghosts in search of the living. It was a dilapidated mess that even the most desperate thief would ignore. The only secure aspect was the door: a slab of oak carved and padlocked to please a prince. I greeted the haunted edifice with a wry grin.

"Home at last." Leastwise my newest home. One in a long line of decrepit dwellings. Since my peoples' removal, no house was 'home' for more than two weeks. Once I exhausted a building's resources, I moved onward in an endless cycle of stiff keys and collected dust.

I unlocked the door, shouldering the bulky thing open. Donovan followed me into the shadowed domain, rightfully frightened. He was not alone in that sentiment.

I struck a match, lighting the solitary lamp which hung at eye-level. The darkness receded. Golden light blazed in the deathly hall. Haunted corners became commonplace. Ghosts vanished, replaced by shredded cobwebs. Donovan sidled closer to the lantern. So close, in fact, that his hand brushed my leg. I laughed at his reaction, the sound eerie and overloud in the gloom.

"Sorry about the mess. I moved in last night and

haven't had time to clean up. The kitchen should be this way."

"Should be?" Donovan squeaked. He skittered along beside me, wary of every shadow that dared pollute our sphere of light.

"It'll be alright, Donovan. This house only has four rooms. One is bound to be the kitchen."

Donovan followed my lead, his silence downright judgemental. He doubted my navigational skills almost as acutely as I did. Choosing the likeliest door, I flung it open. A table, unlit wood stove, and an assortment of cupboards met my gaze. I sighed, relieved.

"See? Kitchen."

"Lucky guess," Donovan hmphed. He sounded more like a grouchy troll than a young boy. He slumped in a dusty chair, crossing his arms upon the table. A fresh layer of grime coated his lanky limbs. He sighed. 'Twas an intentional, overloud burst of air meant to stir both dust and annoyance. It stirred neither.

I held my lamp up to the well-stocked wood stove until the kindling began to smoulder. Life came into the oven. Cold logs burst alight in an array of vibrant flames. In minutes, a cheery fire engulfed the wood.

With the fire tended to, I set about other business.

I rummaged through cupboard after cupboard, selecting whatever food I deemed edible. The mound rose. Donovan's stomach growled. Hands trembling from the weight, I set a cast iron pan on the smouldering woodstove and piled a log upon the emboldened embers. In a matter of minutes, I prepped a plate heaping with eggs, hardtack, and dried fruits.

Donovan hesitated. For a fraction of a second, he merely stared at the food in blatant disbelief. The roundness of his eyes rivalled that of the plate. Seizing his fork, Donovan devoured the provender with a hunger that could only be described as ravenous.

Plate after plate I provided for him. I stirred porridge, fried eggs, and sliced fruit until my pantry was all but depleted. Not that it held much to begin with. Most of the food was rotten, and the rest meticulously preserved by whoever lived there before me.

Half an hour passed in this manner. I served my guest in silence. He ate whatever I provided with unparalleled gusto. At length, Donovan paused. Slow and deliberate, he swallowed his final bite. A sickly pallor stole over his face.

"It's poisoned," he murmured, wiping porridge from his blanched lips. I cocked an eyebrow. Genuine curiosity sparked in my heart.

"What gave you that idea?" I asked.

"You aren't eating."

"I'm not hungry."

"You said earlier that breakfast wouldn't make itself."

"I never said whose breakfast, did I?"

Donovan froze, then reddened. Anger glinted clear and wild in his ever-expressive eyes. Fuming, he stabbed the table. Dishes clattered as the wood split about his fork. Violence shivered in his shrivelled muscles. Raw, animalistic violence.

"You tricked me!" he spat.

I wiped the spittle from my face and sighed. My petty annoyance seemed laughable compared to the betrayal in his voice.

"Can you blame me?" I asked.

"Yes."

"I tricked you, to that I will confess, but you are better off because of it. Now, you have a full stomach and a clear mind. Two things you did not have before we met."

Donovan glared. His wordless contempt stung to say the least. To say the most…suffice it to say my grief nearly shattered its Vial.

"Donovan, I understand you don't like strangers. I am not overfond of them myself, but not everyone you meet is evil. We've had more than our fair share of bad experiences. I see that, and I won't ask for any details, but whatever happened, please consider me an exception."

"Hah! Really? What bad people did you meet?" Donovan snorted, knuckles white as he clutched the fork.

"It doesn't matter anymore."

"I say it does."

Anger. Grief. Resentment. Sorrow. Each flared within their respective Vials. It ached for me to control them all. There were so many. So, so many burdens to shoulder. I drew a long, steadying breath.

"They left, Donovan. They are never coming back. I will *never* need to worry about them again."

"Liar."

I flinched. Inside my satchel, a Vial cracked. Sorrow bathed the contents of my pack. Anger brimmed, not far behind. Calm stole over me. Unnatural, cold, barren, calm.

"The town speaks for me. Did you see anyone in the street?"

"It's early."

"Not that early."

"Why should I believe a random hermit like you? You're barely more than a child yourself yet you pretend to be some all-knowing adult," Donovan sneered. My innards twisted. Sorrow dripped from my satchel in turquoise streams. *He's hurting, Wey. He doesn't mean it. He doesn't mean it.*

"You have no one else to trust."

"I have *no one* to trust. End of story. Last time I trusted someone I ended up enslaved."

Donovan scraped the grime from his wrists and neck. Scabs, blood-encrusted and riddled with putrescence, infected his calloused flesh. My sorrow gushed. Within its confines, anger creaked. How could someone harm Donovan? Let alone enslave him! The wounded boy shot to his feet. Fury blazed in his glassy, brown eyes.

"You're in league with them. You are. They sent you to trick me and I fell for it."

Before I could speak, Donovan dashed past me. He stumbled across warped floorboards and lunged for the nearest door handle. The storage room.

"Donovan, no!"

The door flew open. My heart plummeted.

Hundreds of sturdy Vials rolled across the threshold. Their faint light filled the kitchen with an eerie glow. My burdens deflated as I felt all my emotions blank. Vials lined the room beyond. Every surface, shelf, and cupboard was rank with them. Bottle and stopper. Glass and cork. Donovan stared. What more could he do?

"What is this?" Donovan breathed. I stepped forward, daring to rest a hand upon his shoulder.

"My people are never coming back. They left me to care for their burdens. Someone needed to go down with the ship so that everyone else might escape." The confession lifted a weight from my heart. Resentment burbled. Whether it grew or shrank I could not discern. Donovan stiffened beneath my grip. His body quivered. Hot tears cut ravines in the dirt on his cheeks. He shoved my hand aside and turned, eyes wild with rage once again.

"How could they do that to you?"

I shrugged, unable to meet that frantic gaze. "It no longer matters."

"I don't understand. Why aren't you angry?" he screamed.

"I am."

"That—" Donovan jabbed an accusatory finger at my chest. "—isn't angry! You should be screaming, crying, breaking your head against the furniture. You shouldn't be so...so..."

"Quiet?" I supplied.

"Yes! How can you be so quiet? They abandoned you."

"They chose me."

"You were a tool. A way out. They used you!"

"I *let* them use me, Donovan," I sighed, tension welling in my chest. A numbness dulled my voice, quieting it further. Donovan pressed claw-like hands over his temples, gritting his teeth until they squeaked.

"Why?" he demanded. Such a small word for such a complicated question.

"Because I love them." The whispered admission ground the shattered remnants of my heart into a powder.

Silent tears begged for release, only to be blinked into submission. Sorrow and truth hung in the air between us. Love undeserved and unrequited freely given regardless. With the truth spoken, I finally allowed my tears to fall.

"They didn't love you back," Donovan grumbled.

"I know, but I think…" I fought the tears, determined to overpower the lump in my throat. "I think I can forgive them."

"They don't deserve your forgiveness."

"That's the beauty of it."

"Beauty?" Donovan blazed. "I see no beauty, only pain. They betrayed you!"

"They did, and it hurts, but I can't hold onto my anger forever."

Donovan crossed his atrophied arms and grumbled, "I can."

"Donovan, when you bottle up any emotion, especially anger, you must let out and let go of a little at a time. If you don't, you will explode. I saw it all the time among my people. All the time. You need to let go."

A bitter, sulky expression encompassed Donovan's mood. His wild eyes shifted. As he sighed, his gaze grew docile. Tame and thoughtful. I caught a faint glimmer of the true Donovan in that gaze. The Donovan before his slavery.

"You aren't talking about your people anymore," he said. Observant of him. I shook my head.

The boy's scowl melted into something soft. Something complacent. Tears of rage gentled. In a risky venture, I spread my arms wide. I offered a smile as teasing as it was inviting. *You know you want it,* the smile coaxed.

Donovan rushed into the hug. No bitterness or hesitation required. The once-hateful child sobbed into my embrace. I held him in silence.

"I forgive you, Weylin," he whispered. "I forgive your people, and I forgive *them*. Can—can I stay here? I don't want to go home. Please, Wey?"

I chuckled, hoping he couldn't hear the tears in my voice. "I think that's the first time anyone has called me Wey."

Donovan clutched me tighter in reply.

"Of course. You can stay."

Neither of us moved for a long while. Stillness drifted into the house like a fogbank. Birds rested curiously on shutter and windowsill. Their subdued chirrups hardly disturbed the sudden quietude. Apple blossoms fluttered by as the wind tore them from their trees and drove them abroad. Delicate violets studded the cobblestones outside, blessing us with their raspberry-esque scent. Donovan himself smelled of birch, mud, and sweat. Not an altogether unpleasant aroma if it weren't for the hint of infection about it.

"Can you feel them all? The Vials?" he asked at length. My grip slackened and I nodded, the immense weight fresh upon my mind.

Donovan ducked out of my loosened hold. Slowly, he backed into the cluttered storage room. Vials rolled. Glass crunched against dust and grit. Donovan took one in his hand. 'Twas a small thing, perfectly round and brimming with self-loathing.

He smashed it on the ground.

An abrupt ache stabbed my chest, followed by my belated scream. I stumbled. My fingers curled around the doorframe for support. I swayed as if on hinges, clutching the pained area. A heaviness receded from my soul. My self-loathing lessened.

"Did it help?" Donovan asked. I nodded, hardly able to breathe for the shock of it, let alone speak.

"Good."

A sickly blend of dread and elation blossomed in my chest. For a moment, I feared said blend would leak through my shirt and stain the floor. I watched, mute with blissful horror, as Donovan pried a narrow shelf from its moorings. The shelf's contents shattered when they fell. I felt each burden leave my heart. They broke into a thousand fragments and soaked through crevices in the wood to seek the fallow ground below. The soil devoured it. Hungrily. Greedily. Instantly.

Donovan seized the shelf and proceeded to smash every last Vial. Only the ones within my satchel remained intact. Unfamiliar emotions welled within my soul. Foremost were gratitude and confusion. I slumped against the doorframe, numb. Huddled into the tightest position manageable and stared blankly at the wall.

Everything slipped away. Anxiety, grief, anger, sorrow. Emotions not originally my own forsook me to become one with the loam. All my cares streamed away, superseded by nothingness. I felt drained. Drained of my burdens and surrendered to oblivion.

With his task done, Donovan knelt before me. Fresh ichor stained where glass protruded from his feet. Between the two of us, his eyes were the more docile.

"You…" I swallowed, the words meek and insignificant compared to Donovan's deed. "You set me free."

Donovan made a face somewhat reminiscent of a smile.

"Just returning the favour. I have something else to return as well."

"What?" I asked, breaths shallow and uneven. The boy shuffled closer. His eyes glinted mischievously.

"This." Donovan ensnared me in a hug long before I had a chance to blink. Heartbeats overlapped. Breaths intertwined as our chests heaved in unison. He held me. I held him. Misery faded into a distant memory.

In a crash of tears and hitching sobs, I realized I was not abandoned after all.

The moment, however sweet, was short-lived. A far-off sound penetrated the stillness. A sound half-forgotten and wholly unwelcome: hounds.

Donovan went rigid in my grasp. His heart pounded rapidly against my own. Terror froze him in place. Angered shouts intermingled with the hounds' baying. They were on the scent. *Donovan's* scent.

Men and beasts tore through the deserted streets. The cobbles rang with their thunderous approach. We had seconds before the hunters found their prey.

Donovan shrieked, burying his face in the tatters of my scarf. A chill wind swept through wall and window, augmenting his fear. Frantic, I surrendered thought to instinct and sprinted into the storage room with Donovan in my arms. Vials crunched beneath my boots. Fragments stuck in the leather, sole and side alike. I ignored the barbs, prodding broken glass aside to clear a Donovan-sized patch in the debris.

I set my new burden atop a cupboard. He trembled, every limb quivering. Cupping his cheek, I coaxed him to meet my gaze. His frenzied eyes met my assumed calm. False tranquility failed to undo the knots in my stomach. It did, however, undo some of the tension in his.

"Stay here and don't move an inch until I say so. Alright?" Donovan nodded, pale and speechless with fright. Despite the early hour, the shadows seemed to stretch forward to shield him. A phenomenon few heard of and seldom saw. Castiel's blessing.

Dogs howled outside the front door. Fist pounded wood. Donovan cowered, shrinking into the shadows as muffled demands filtered through the door. I left him there: a terrified child in a chamber of shattered burdens. The latch locked with a gentle *click*. I wound through the dark hallway, lantern in hand. The assailants knocked with renewed vigour. Growls crawled up and down my spine as I turned the knob.

Get it over with, Weylin. The sooner you let them in, the sooner you can throw them out.

The hinges never had a chance to creak. Four men burst into my domain, hounds at their heels. I bristled. Indignation morphed into resentment in a trice. The men's shrewd eyes, casual sneers, and readied fists betrayed their nature. At a single glance, I knew those men were cruel. Yet their cruelty seemed more a decision than a trait. One man shoved me aside, keeping a firm hold on my scarf as he did. Whether I liked it or not, they were in my house, and I was at their mercy.

"Where is the boy?" the man demanded.

"Personally, I consider myself a youth."

"Don't be coy!" He jerked my scarf. The fabric coiled tighter about my neck, chafing the skin. "We're looking for a fugitive. A young boy. About waist high and bound to be a bit scraggly by now. The scent leads to your house. Have you seen him?"

"No."

The brute held my face so near to his I could smell his breath. It reeked of I knew not what. Something bitter and rancid that caused my stomach to churn.

Hounds growled at me in tandem, snuffling their way to where I stood. Once they stood within biting distance, they paused and snarled. Several of them began to howl. My heart leapt into my throat. The man yanked me closer. His death grip on my scarf intensified. His companions chuckled.

"The dogs say you lie."

"Dogs can't talk."

A terrible jerk on my neck hoisted me off the ground. The man slammed me against the wall. Stars dazzled my eyes as skull met wood. Dust fell in a deluge. Cobwebs descended to coat the four hunters. I clutched the strangling fabric above my collarbone, determined never to wear a scarf again. The man, obviously their leader, leaned in until his eyes were level with mine.

"We know he's here, Weylin. You and your people are terrible liars. You have two options: tell us where you're hiding him, or we *persuade* you to tell us."

He sounded ominously fond of the second option.

The lead hunter tossed me aside. My ribs and arm connected with the floor at an odd angle, sending jolts of pain through every bone in question. I coughed and gagged, tearing the scarf from my neck. Phantom pain persisted. The men loomed over me. One of the lesser hunters feigned unclasping a hound's leash. Shaking, I scrambled to my knees. A threatening hand seized my shoulder. The leader.

"Talk," he ordered.

Do it for Donovan, I reminded myself. *He needs you to trick them. He needs you to stay calm.*

"I…I'll give you the tour. Try to avoid any broken glass."

"That's not what we asked, boy," the hound keeper barked. He appeared nearly as canine as his pets, teeth sharp and eyes vicious. I stood, dusting off my clothes with morbid composure. All my fear manifested within the fortified confines of my satchel.

"This way."

I led them opposite the kitchen into the bedroom. Two broken banisters, a torn curtain, and a ramshackle dresser adorned the chamber. Molding blankets slouched off the ragged mattress. Dust motes polluted the air. If I had not discarded my scarf, I would have pressed it securely against my face to breathe. That said, I did not breathe at all.

The hunters demolished the furniture. They reduced my pitiable bed to a rubbish heap. Dresser became firewood. Rubble coated the floor and pervaded the atmosphere. I flinched, standing as far from the havoc as the hand on my shoulder allowed.

"Stalling will not save him," their leader said. His eyes, a startling deep brown, bore into my soul. My posture straightened. I refused to let the man intimidate me.

Donovan's safety demanded it.

"Then it's a good thing I have nothing to hide."

"We will see."

"Will you?" I turned to confront the bestial hunter. My stance mirrored his own. Strong and unwavering. Beyond that, not a single trait connected us. He was stocky, tall, and muscular. I was small and lank to a degree that would concern most mothers. Fine clothing hugged his form. Rags swathed my body in a multitude of haphazard layers. I resisted out of love. He persisted out of hate. There we stood, opposites in every way save one: neither of us would bend.

My defiance was met by a backhanded slap.

"Don't play games with me! Back there. What is that room?"

"The kitchen," I replied, probing the assaulted area.

"And beyond it?"

"Vials. Hundreds of them."

"Yours?"

"Everyone's. The Vials of every Weylin from here to the North Sea are in that room."

The hunter blinked away his shock with unparalleled nonchalance. He crossed his arms, furnishing me with a false sense of freedom.

"Sounds like an ideal place to hide a runaway," he said. I forced a laugh, the sound weak and dry. Good. The more he underestimated me the better.

"That runaway would need to be smaller than a cork to fit in there. Every time I open the door, an avalanche greets me. Search at your own risk."

Indecision poisoned the confidence in his gaze.

That's it. Question. Wonder. Am I innocent? Am I a liar? Did your dogs smell Donovan or the Vials?

"The kitchen," he growled. "Show it to me."

"Gladly."

The dogs yipped and bayed, bounding ahead of me. They streaked into the kitchen and immediately began pawing at the storage room door. Evidently, they were much keener than their brutish counterparts. Keener of both sense and mind, in my humble opinion.

Fear creaked against its confines. Rather than panic, I methodically emptied the contents of my satchel. Vial after Vial. One emotion at a time. I set each on the table alongside Donovan's half-used dishware. The cloying dregs of sorrow smeared my hands. Infernal stuff. Hours of painstaking scrubbing awaited me. *If I even survive. Master of All Worlds, if Donovan and I survive, I will even be grateful for sorrow stains.*

Canine whimpers prickled my ears. One dog sneezed. Many backed away, glass imbedded in their paws. Despite their sinister appearance, I pitied them. The men chose cruelty. Their dogs did not.

Unfortunately, the multitude of broken Vials drew the lead hunter's gaze. His curiosity piqued visibly. In a twinkling, the hunter seized the door handle. My blood froze.

"DON'T!"

The door flew open. Donovan shrieked, tears punctuating his cries. Dogs howled and keened. Hunters cheered. Chaos ruled the city that morning, thrusting me into the very epicentre.

My Vials exploded.

Anger, fear, resentment, and grief erupted in a shower

of glass and liquid gold. Fragments sliced my cheek. Clear missiles stabbed my limbs. I slammed the door on Donovan. Glass pelted the invaders. The physical equivalent of my emotions seeped into their wounds, stinging. It blazed and burned within my cheek, dulled only by the intoxicating flood of adrenaline.

"Get. Out," I ordered. No one moved. Hounds whimpered. Their masters stood in dumb silence. I turned on them, snatching the nearest kitchen utensil. A ladle. I smashed it against the door handle. Latch and ladle broke. Infuriated, I positioned myself between hunter and prey. I brandished my mangled weapon, sharp end foremost. My words came slow, even, and threatening.

"He is neither your property nor your concern. Whatever he did is forgotten. Whoever he was no longer matters. Now, get out!"

The men fled. Blood splattered the space they once occupied in ruddy pools. Chastened hounds followed close on their heels. I lowered my impromptu weapon, probing the gash on my cheek.

That one is bound to scar, I thought. Apparently, I had regained enough presence of mind to register annoyance. The door creaked open behind me. A trembling form huddled against my leg. Rather than ask, 'are they gone?' or offer a polite, 'thank you, Weylin,' Donovan said, "You threatened them with a ladle?"

"Quiet you," I huffed, half breathless. Donovan responded with a shaky hug. I returned the embrace, feeling the adrenaline abandon my body to exhaustion.

"Thank you," he whispered.

"My pleasure. Those brutes tangled with the wrong

boys this time."

I glanced down at my new responsibility, daring to stroke his hair.

"Did you step on any glass?"

Donovan shook his head. "Not that I know of."

"Alright, but just to be sure, let's have a look at those feet."

Muse of the Mountain

Not long ago, in lands I know well, the enchantment of music changed my life forever.

An eerie clicking resounded in the mountains that night. I paused, resting a hand against the strings of my lyre. The embers of an evening fire crinkled in the hearth. Zemira's blessing seemed to linger o'er the dying coals, preserving their warmth. They clinked and crackled in time with the mysterious tick in the distance. Silence, then a click. Over and over until there was only silence. The birds ceased their singing. The world stilled.

A haunting melody broke through the quietude The dissonant ring of a waltz in A minor, the simplest minor of all, surrounded my mountain home. Eerie and ancient, yet sweet and near at hand; my heart swelled at the sound.

My ever-attentive ears knew it to be the chime of a music box. I groped for my cane. My heart drifted toward the music. In the natural blackness, my fingers brushed the ornate carvings of my staff. Carvings of dragons, gems, and musical notes circled the mahogany cane in an endless loop while its distinctive scent tickled my nose. As I leaned on it, the staff became something akin to my eyes. The woollen shawl slipped from my shoulder, dragging on the floor.

"Tina? Why did you stop?" my sister groaned. Narah's bedstead creaked as she raised her body in question.

"Do you hear that?" I breathed, hardly capable of speech for the wonder of it.

"Hear what?" Narah yawned. She rolled over on her mat of straw and fur. How could she not hear the music? How could she not recognize its beauty?

"A music box! Listen."

Narah listened on the brink of slumber. Before long, she snuggled deep into her mound of bedcoverings and sighed.

"You're imagining things again. Try to…" Gentle snores drifted through the low cottage.

Sleep, I finished in my mind. *Try to sleep.*

Should I? Should I pretend to hear nothing and sleep it away? I wondered. The music might not be there by morning.

Although I tried, I could not ignore the call. Dangers lurked in the mountains of our homeland. Perils beyond my knowledge, imagination, and sight. Perhaps the music belonged to said perils. Or perhaps…it was meant for me to follow.

*Maybe just a little way up…*I decided. Swallowing my

fear, I cinched the ends of my shawl to my bronze wristlets and strode into the night. A midnight breeze caressed my cheek, blowing the bangs from my forehead. The varnished wood of my lyre swiftly absorbed the cold. I strapped it to my belt and stumbled onto the lush ledge surrounding my home. High above me, someone rewound the music box.

I blindly traversed the path ascending the mountain's summit. As I climbed, the temperature plummeted. Wisps of snow entangled themselves in my braid. I blinked unseeing eyes as the snow danced about the tassels of my shawl and tattered hem of my dress, wishing I could see it. Mud splashed my boots and staff as weariness slowed my pace. I pressed on toward the glorious melody. Nothing, neither weather nor fatigue, would deter me.

As the owner of the music box twisted its key in a series of echoing clicks, I unlatched my lyre and imitated the mysterious waltz. I copied it to perfection. The gentle melody rang across the Copper Mountains, the strings of my lyre coming to life beneath my fingertips. The clicks ceased. Curious hesitation lurked behind the silence. I renewed their song, hoping for them to take up the air once more.

The music resumed. Never again did it cease, even to rewind, until I reached a lush cave carved into the peak. The scent of flowers and fertile ground filled my nostrils, defying the layers of snow heaped just beyond the cave's parameters. Someone breathed farther inside the cave. Strong, even, healthy breaths. The unmistakable sound of wings tickled my ears.

They seized the instrument's key, halting the tune.

Slowly, they wound the key. Fabric rustled and grass bent as they set the box on the ground. The melody returned. I strummed a matching series of notes. In a swipe and a click, the creature tucked the key away.

"You can hear me," he concluded, his voice as melodious as that of his box. "Can you see me as well?"

"No, I…I cannot see. I'm blind. But I am not imagining things…am I?"

"I should hope not. I like to believe we both exist." The boy chuckled, his warm grin spreading from his heart to mine. I stepped into the thriving enclosure. As if by magic, the warmth of summer enveloped me. Feathers shuffled as the boy stood and bowed. I heard the tip of a wing graze the floor. I bent my knees, offering a polite dip of my head.

"Anadil Fintan, at your service. You must be the musician my master sent me to find."

"Musician?" I breathed. I dared not think he meant me.

"You are Valentina Enid, aren't you?"

"Yes."

"Muse of the Mountain my people call you. My master composed this melody for you. If you'll follow me, he would like to hear you play."

Muse of the Mountain? I thought. My heart fluttered. To play before one who composed such a melody would be an honour. More than that. It would be a dream come true! Even still…

"My family—" I began, reluctant.

"—will be none the wiser," Anadil interrupted. "I can have you back at your cottage in a matter of hours."

Anadil took my hand. Hesitant, I received his touch. I felt him bow once again. His fingers closed around mine as he planted a gentlemanly kiss on my knuckles. Anadil scooped up his music box with a noisy flourish, wrapped both arms around me, and flew into the ivy wall of the cave. I gasped as tangling vines gave way to open air.

Time and music became tangible, as well as the emotions that accompanied them. Anadil radiated a joyous rhythm. The subdued beat of wonder enshrined me in a living minuet. Fragrant flowers, sulfurous mountains, and salted seas soared by. Anadil bypassed them all. I longed to stop and touch each verdant leaf, but alas, Anadil flew faster than a dragon.

* * *

Something powerful loomed in the near distance, its own rhythm alerting me to its presence. The mysterious bulk thrummed with elegance and light.

"There's our stop, Miss Enid," Anadil called, his voice diminished by the wind. "A palace of diamonds grander than the glistening sea."

"Tina!" I insisted. "Call me Tina!"

"Beg pardon?" Anadil shouted in confusion. Close as we were, my words vanished in the mighty zephyr. Anadil, whatever creature he was, shrugged and carried on.

We flew to a flat-topped turret where a multitude of feathers rustled in anticipation. A flock of Anadil's people awaited there. Winged creatures of every voice, pitch, and emotion gathered to greet us. A polonaise of curiosity hung over the throng, sped by their aforementioned anticipation. Anadil lowered me to the dais, hovering to hold me erect. I gradually brought my cane to the platform. If I knew for certain what material composed the glorious castle, I might not have been so fearful. Whatever it was clinked mightily beneath my staff and possessed no definitive scent. Crystal perhaps?

With each solid *clack*, I cringed, worried the floor would give way beneath me. Anadil walked at my side. He politely folded one arm beneath mine and a wing over my shoulder. The boy smelled of mocha and feathers, his hair especially. His bare arms pulsed in confidence and pleasure as he led me to an auditorium of stone. The clink of my cane transitioned to a dull clomp as the air grew damp. A slight metallic taint tickled my tongue. Rock scraped beneath wood. The odours of various minerals pervaded my nostrils while I drew a deep, lingering breath. I rested my hand on an ornate, lacquered railing.

Anxious butterflies bombarded my stomach. Apprehension thrummed across my skin as steadily as waves upon the seashore. Anadil rested a hand on the crook of my arm. Somehow, I knew his rhythm meant empathy. The kind soul gave my arm a squeeze.

"May I carry you the rest of the way, Miss Enid? The stairs are bothersome even to us flying folk," he offered. For a moment, I considered it. Flight was so simple. So quick. However, I was not an invalid, and the stairs were nothing compared to the mountain I scaled earlier that evening.

"Thank you, but no. I prefer to walk."

Anadil hummed, consenting to my wishes. Odd. Few people allowed my independence so readily.

"If I may, Miss…" Anadil began, clearing his throat. His rhythm hitched, disrupting the ambience. "What happened to your eyes?"

I blinked, slow and methodical as I savoured the silence. Over the years I had lost track of how many people asked me that exact same question. Despite the temptation to concoct a tale of danger and heroism, I always responded with the same age-old truth.

"I was born this way."

"Then your other senses must be incredible!" Anadil exclaimed. I laughed, drinking in his thoughtful tone. We descended into a contemplative silence. Tune and tempo faded for our convenience. Time flowed about us in a continuous stream. A stage of sanded wood met us at the crest of the carpeted, marble staircase.

"Anadil, what exactly are you?" I asked, too curious to hold my tongue. Anadil indulged in an infectious chuckle.

"Some call me a faerie, a fae, or simply a winged-one but most refer to me as an angel. I won't tell you who is wrong, of course. To you, Miss Enid, I am a friend. My master knows who and what I am. Nothing else matters."

I had never met a man more content with his identity. Anadil's master knew who he was, and that sufficed. I envied his confidence. If only I told others who I was and was not with such certainty!

The steady clomp of staff against stone shifted to the comfortable cadence of wood on wood. I drew a long breath and allowed the sweetly rugged scent of mahogany to pervade my nostrils. 'Twas the aroma that guided my steps nearly all my life, forming both cane and lyre. It enriched my senses as little else could.

As we crossed the dais, excitement spurred Anadil's pulse. Swaths of cinnamon-scented fabric brushed my arm as he drew back a silken curtain with a flourish. The veil closed behind us with a hiss. Confident footsteps filled the space before me, disrupting the near silence. A man hummed in thought as the steps came to a standstill. Before he spoke, I felt his voice warm my heart. His simple *"welcome, child"* gifted me all the love and acceptance I ever hoped for.

"Valentina Enid, it is my pleasure to introduce you to the Master of All Worlds," Anadil proclaimed.

"Welcome, Valentina," the Master greeted. Kindness radiated from his rich tone. "It is an honour to finally meet you."

"The—the honour is mine…sir." I fumbled to perform some semblance of a curtsy. The Master chuckled, cupping my cheek in his hand. Although I knew him not, the action seemed natural. The Master responded in tune with the comfort I experienced.

"No need for formalities. You may call me Spirit." Spirit paused and stepped away, squeezing my hand in invitation. "If I am not mistaken, you have something to play for us."

"Of course, Spirit. What would you like me to play?"

"Your song, Valentina," Spirit urged. I undid the clasp about my lyre. My cane nearly clattered to the ground as I relaxed my grip.

"I don't have one." Shame blazed in my cheeks. How could I play a song that didn't exist? Worse, how could I disappoint the Master? I—

A hand clasped my shoulder. Spirit lifted my quivering

chin. No touch ever had, or ever would, equal the kindness his exuded. His gentleness washed over me. As it did, the tune dwindled to the softest lullaby in existence and beyond. Peace.

"Everyone has a song, my dear. What is yours?"

Reassurance coursed through me. I stood taller, despite my diminutive height. Neither lack of sight nor stature inhibited me. Spirit trusted me. He knew my song. In time, I would know it as well.

"Here is a hint," Anadil offered, pressing a wooden box into the palm of my hand. The music box.

"Your music box," Spirit corrected within my mind. His words, although sudden, were not invasive. In fact, he belonged there. I knew he belonged in my thoughts as assuredly as he belonged on that stage. With his words and my melody swirling in my mind, I rested on a nearby stool and began to play.

A steady minor strain rose from the strings of my lyre. At first soft and melancholy, the music swelled. The piece morphed and changed into a lilting rhythm of joy and pain. Peace and foreboding fraught the thrumming of my instrument. A mingled melody of constancy, change, and calm resounded throughout the auditorium.

Anadil's kin flooded the stadium in a flurry of wings, loath to disturb the music. The soft rustling of feathers and clothes brushed my ears, doing little to distract me. Their quiet wonder sent butterflies rippling through my stomach. I shifted in my seat, swaying to the rhythm. The waltz, solemn and haunting, finished on a triumphant Tiers de Picardie. From minor to major in the smoothest of transitions.

Cheers erupted from the winged crowd. I jumped at the noise, sending my cane clattering to the stage. The joyous shouts rose above its hollow thump. Anadil soared amid the ruckus. His voice faded in the clamour, drowned out by that of his kin. To my surprise, Spirit cheered loudest of all.

Before the applause could fade, Spirit silenced himself and approached me. He radiated with approval and the scent of lilacs. I offered a slight bow from where I sat. With a chuckle, Spirit dropped to his knees and wrapped his arms around me.

"Well done, Valentina. You have an amazing gift. Use it well," he whispered, his words sweet as honey as they brushed past my ear.

"I will, Spirit," I promised. Tears prickled my unseeing eyes as I returned that warmest of hugs. "I will."

Slow and reluctant, the winged creatures filtered out of the auditorium, leaving a peaceful quietude in their wake. Hums of appreciation lingered in the rows of seats. Anadil descended. His wings twitched noisily, fluttering as if they were marionettes controlled by his heartstrings. Taking my hand, he dipped forward in an elegant bow.

"Anadil Fintan, ready to fly you home, Miss Enid, as promised."

"Already?" The word rushed from my mouth before I could stop it. Spirit offered a benign laugh. He pressed my hand in his, gifting me courage, comfort, and hope. If only he could be with me at all hours.

"I *am* with you, Valentina. Sometimes you may not see me, but I will always watch over you. Remember this."

I gently squeezed his hand and rose, gripping my cane.

"Always," I vowed. Spirit bowed to me, and I heard him step away. Cautious hands encircled my waist, lifting me above the fragrant stage of wood. The delightfully sickening sensation of flight coiled about the pit of my stomach. Spirit's warmth followed Anadil and I as we soared out of the amphitheatre of stone.

Time flowed ever onwards as we flew above the land. A land of truth, transparency, and love. A land of winged companions and crystal castles. A land unlike any in my home, fantasies, or dreams. One I would always cherish in my memories. As we travelled, I plucked absent-mindedly at the strings of my lyre. My fingers danced across the strands, emitting a mournful farewell.

My lament merged with the onward current of time, the strain practically coming to life in a soulful dirge.

Loss. Loss permeated my sorrowful tune.

All too soon, Anadil passed through that lush gateway upon the mountain's summit. Down the mountainside we went, hovering inches above the well beaten path. A deep, restful silence enveloped us as we descended. Dawn rose cold and brilliant on the mountain. His rays followed us down the slope in a friendly game of chase, swift yet never quick enough to nip Anadil's wings. A heady breeze giggled and twirled about us, catching our clothes in playful gusts.

At last, my fingers caressed the knobby wooden door to my home. Although it was no diamond palace, it was mine and I loved it dearly. Wind whistled through chinks in the evergreen logs. No doubt the breeze wreaked mischief on the dying embers within.

Anadil set me on the warped porch before my cabin.

The rising sun warmed our cheeks with his cheeriest rays as we fluttered to the ground. Anadil pressed something small and solid into my hands. As he continued to clasp my closed fingers, I knew what laid inside: the key to my music box.

"Miss Enid, would you play for us again someday?" Anadil asked, his voice low and hesitant. I felt him peer at me with inquisitive eyes. I smiled, not wanting the moment to end.

"Of course," I assured him, "but how will I get there? I cannot fly."

Anadil's ever-expressive wings quivered in excitement. Gradually, his hands slipped from mine as he spread his feathered pinions.

"You need only whisper for us. Whether into the dancing breeze or singing embers, we will listen. Whenever you feel alone, play your lyre, for one of us will always be there to hear it. If you doubt me, play by your hearth tomorrow evening and I will come."

Truth saturated his words. Even if I wanted to doubt him, I could not. Anadil ascended, his wings beating the air in graceful strokes.

"I will, and please, call me Tina."

The sun blazed bright and triumphant on my blind eyes. His warmth shifted as Anadil's shadow drifted across my face in yet another bow.

"As you wish, Miss Tina!" he called.

That night, I sat alone and unhindered by the flames of the hearth. Narah, mother, and father retired to bed hours earlier. Silence and remembrance were my faithful companions. Not a dust bunny stirred in the stillness. I listened to the waning embers, my mind straying to a land above the mountain and beyond an ivy veil. Gently, I strummed my song across the ever-responsive strings of my lyre.

A kind voice spoke at my side.

"You called, Miss Tina?"

* * *

Every night I played melody upon melody for Anadil and Spirit. Every night they listened. Sometimes I journeyed beyond The Mountain Gate, as I began to call it. Most days, however, they came to me. Although I strummed numerous pieces and songs, they never grew weary of "Tina's Song." One of them requested it each night without fail. Both loved it deeply, wordless though it was.

Perhaps one day I would find words to accompany my melody. Until then, the notes spoke for themselves.

They have ever since.

A Tale of Three Roses

The following tale will make no sense whatsoever unless you first realize this: a white rose means purity, yellow means friendship, and a blue rose symbolizes mystery and intrigue.

That being said, let us begin.

Once, there lived three roses, though not the kind you might think. These roses were young women of a particularly powerful bloodline. Half faerie and half human. Their names were Bianca, Solasta, and Azure. Bianca of the pearl hair. Solasta, blessed with golden skin. Azure graced by her sapphire eyes. I simply called them roses because it suited them.

These three girls lived by themselves in a cottage along the western shore of Melian. Their home was a peaceful sort of place where the loudest sound anyone made was laughter. Squabbles happened, as they always do, but all were resolved with time.

Bianca wandered the cliffs, Solasta the forest, and Azure the shoals. Each loved their respective haunts yet never lost sight of their dear little cottage. This may surprise you, but not a one of them knew what a rose was. Not until I wandered into their lives.

Yes, me. A golden-eyed wanderer without home or destination. My name, believe it or not, was Anonymous. Anonymous Finchley, to be precise.

I rolled nonchalantly into their domain, as I rolled everywhere in those days. A wayfaring young lass as listless as I was hungry and hungry as I was fatigued. Not that I would ever admit to such a thing. Monster hunters seldom do. *Especially* monster hunters on a mission.

It was a placid morning the day I arrived. One permeated by birdsong and rosy sunshine to the point where even a devout night owl conceded to its majesty. Golden hay bent in the beginnings of a sultry summer breeze. Grasses rustled and giggled around their taller, straw neighbours. Wispy clouds flitted o'er the blue heavens. Ah yes, 'twas a good day to be alive.

The path I wandered rattled beneath my wheeled chair. The loose cobbles jarred and bumped until my teeth ached. Pulling myself forward on mangled toes, I drank in the scenery. Serene. Peaceful. Painless. Untainted by monster lust. I sniffed the air to be sure. Skeptical as always, I eyed the clear breeze for any tell-tale signs of foul magic. Or Verve, as the inhabitants of Zander dubbed it.

The faintest strand of black Verve wound into the distance.

Well, at least I know he came this way, I thought, examining the trace.

"Greetings, traveller!" called a sunny voice. My hands curled about the bow upon my lap, swiftly nocking an arrow.

"Greetings," I hollered back, scanning the forest in search of the speaker. A resplendent glimmer announced my visitor. Faerie magic enshrined her in an amicable warmth akin to the sun himself. I relaxed my posture and bowstring. It was fortunate I hadn't seized my axe.

As the faerie girl approached, I caught the distinct outline of undeveloped wings. Mere shadows, really. The ephemeral shade of a thing yet to exist. Of all my travels, never had I met such a rosy being. She practically was a rose herself.

"How's all with ye?" Sunshine asked, her accent as light and lilting as her invisible wings.

"Fairly well, and you?"

"Oh, I'm practically blossoming in this weather. Have ye ever felt sich life in the air?"

Most definitely faerie blood in those veins of hers, I concluded. *Can she sense Verve as well?*

"Yes," I said slowly, releasing my weapons as surreptitiously as possible. "A fine morning indeed."

"Me sisters and I were jist having a bit o' a preamble afore breakfast. Ye're welcome t' join us if ye like."

Sunshine offered an impossibly radiant grin. The strengthening sunlight bounded off her skin in playful rays. Friendly Verve swirled about her. An innocent temptation if ever there was one. I nodded, curt and firm.

"I would be delighted." My prey was leagues ahead of

me. A small delay couldn't hurt.

Sunshine bounced on her toes. Sparks flew from her delicate hands as she clapped. Somehow, she failed to notice them.

"Magnificent! Here, let me get that for ye," she said, reaching for the high, sword-notched back of my wheeled chair. I held out a hand, forceful. Pure thunder clouded my expression in juxtaposition to her clear-skied appearance.

"Ho no, no, no. I can push or pull myself as I please, thank you very much. I'd rather stick my head in a beehive than add atrophy to injury. Believe me when I say the exercise does me good."

The faerie girl abruptly dropped her hands. She folded them into the most adroit posture possible, outdoing many nobles of her race.

"Of course. I meant no offence. Beggin' yer pardon, miss. Allow me to start o'er. Me name is Solasta, wanderer of forests and lover of sunlight. I would be mich obliged if ye would join me family in breaking our fast."

I bowed from my seat. "Anonymous Finchley. Bow master, axe wielder, and monster hunter. I gladly accept your invitation."

We traversed the pathway to her home in relative silence. Solasta walked at a slow and thoughtful plod. I pulled myself along by my toes, only resorting to rolling the wheels when absolutely necessary. How else would I maintain the muscles in my legs?

When we arrived, awe washed over me in tangible waves. I felt, saw, and heard the gentle Verve around the cottage. Such love. Such joy. Such serenity. Knowing me, it would likely dissolve into chaos before noontide. Even still, I absorbed the tranquility with eager breaths.

A shock of white hair burst through the shutters. Pearl-studded wings wreathed a young woman's shoulders, vague and insubstantial as a summer mist. I saw them. The girls did not. Such was my blessing and curse. Duality at its finest.

Pearlhead waved enthusiastically through the window. Innocence pure as snowdrops permeated her motions. A second rose.

"Set an extra plate, Bianca, we have a visitor," Solasta hollered. Pearlhead, Bianca, nodded energetically.

"Good mornin' t' ye, visitor! Come inside," Bianca beckoned. I rolled obediently up the walkway, biting my lip to mask the subsequent fatigue. Flagstones caught my wheels. Jarred to a most unpleasant halt, I gritted my teeth and *heaved* against the obstacle.

It budged. The newfound momentum sent me reeling forward at speeds only I could enjoy.

I paused at the doorstep, followed by a somewhat frazzled Solasta. Her phantom wings flickered in annoyance. An involuntary smirk crept across my countenance. I distorted the expression, warping it into a semi-sweet smile. My gut twisted in sudden abhorrence of what I needed to do next. Not a mite of my hesitation showed. I hoped.

"Ah, see *this* I cannot do on my own. If you have a lattice leading to a window, I could climb that and leave my chair behind, but I am afraid stairs and wheeled chairs do not agree." Without another word, I pressed my palms against the handlebars and hauled myself off the seat. I thumped onto the doorstep, unable to slow my descent.

The air abandoned my lungs in a single puff. Feigning nonchalance, I politely motioned from Solasta to my chair.

"Steps mist be a right nightmare to a bein' on wheels sich as yerself," Solasta mused aloud, bodily lifting my chair to set it even with her threshold. The wood creaked. Axels groaned. Spokes shuddered and squeaked. Nevertheless, my shoddy method of transportation survived. I allowed Solasta to hoist me into the seat, masking my laboured breaths with a lighthearted chuckle. Unfortunately, my acting paled in comparison to my finesse in combat.

"Many…many thanks, Solasta."

"'Tis me pleasure, Miss Finchley."

That's what they all say, Sunshine.

The door swung open from within. A smiling half-faerie greeted me in demure silence. Her eyes, clear and piercing as the heavens above, bored into my soul. Spectral wings akin to frozen clouds adorned her back. Her Verve appeared to shift, muddied by a power I could not discern. She nodded to me.

"Welcome t' our home. I am Azure."

Yet another rose, I marvelled. Although…Azure seemed set apart from her sisters. Strangely dignified. Distant. Otherworldly in the sheer penetration of her gaze. A blue rose indeed.

"Yer eyes. One sees differently than t' other. The gold one is no' natural," she observed.

Solasta groaned, "No' agin, Azure! Let her at least eat before ye read her soul, will ye?"

Solemnly, Azure nodded. They led me into their humble abode. I subconsciously massaged the bone beneath my right eye. The gold eye. Golden Sight. Magic Eyes. Spectral Gaze. Such an oddity went by many names. While it was somewhat natural, Azure struck a chord. In a sense, she saw my Sight.

The cottage was a homey little dwelling. Half-burned candles and patched curtains bespoke contented poverty. Rough furniture neatly bedecked the room. I took in the interior at a single glance. Two rooms and two lofts. Quaint. Comfortable. Far superior to any inn, tavern, or palace I had frequented on my journeys, if only for the simple generosity which permeated it. The roses had nothing yet shared everything.

A hearty aroma wafted from the nearby table. Eggs and preserved meats sizzled. Porridge bubbled in a cast-iron kettle fresh off the hob. It was simple, and by no means a feast, but it reeked of camaraderie.

"Lovely, isn't it?" Azure asked, tone gentle and musing.

"It is."

"Are ye going to tell me how ye gained the Second Sight?"

"No."

"As ye wish," she relented. Interesting.

I rolled my chair across the smooth flooring. My twisted knees fit snugly beneath the tabletop. Chips and nicks marred the ancient wood. I fiddled with the nearest spoon, twirling it. Forcefully, I reminded myself that I was not restless. Peace did not unsettle me. Family never made my skin crawl.

Good Verve does not scare me. Alas, weaknesses are difficult to remember. One who knows only strength forgets weakness. One who knows only weakness forgets strength.

Do not forget either strength or weakness, I told myself. *Forgetting strength cost your reputation. Forgetting weakness cost your legs. Remember them.*

What I had expected to be a quiet, civil meal dissolved into pleasant chaos. Dishes were passed from one hand to the next. Feminine chatter, distribution of chores, and other kindly nonsense consumed conversation. Laughter and groans. Compliments and jibes. Those radiant girls, roses though they be, were siblings to the core. Apparently, my very presence made me one of them.

"Anonymous, could ye help me with the dishes after breakfast?" Azure asked. She cast a half-casual glance my direction, sidelong and meaningful. There was a shrewdness to her gaze. A guile. Something her sisters sorely lacked.

"Leave the lass alone, Az," Bianca cut in, her dainty mouth stuffed with porridge. "She is our guest."

"No, no. I'll gladly lend a hand. Ask for any service and it shall be done."

"What do ye ask in exchange, hunter?" Azure probed, eyes glistening with an ethereal glow.

I shrugged, unceremoniously leaning my elbows on the table. "Food for the day and shelter for the night. No more. No less."

"Done," said the roses in unison. Why they were so eager to have a dangerous rogue in their home I could only guess. Perhaps they were lonely.

Perhaps they need a hunter.

Regardless of reason, I dipped my hands into hot water shortly after the deal was struck. 'Twas an unfamiliar sensation. Water was meant to be cold, frigid even. Not warm. Not comfortable. My hands lingered in the hot, sudsy liquid a moment too long. Long enough to engage Azure's penetrating stare at least. Red tinged my half-elven ears as I began scraping residue off dishes.

"Clever of you," I practically muttered, "singling me out for dish duty without sisters within earshot."

"Not everyone is so conniving, Anon."

"Except for you."

Azure nodded, unsmiling. "Except for me."

For the next while we scrubbed in silence. Pots, platters, and serving plates passed reverently through my hands. Gentle wear and tear attested to extensive use and love. Chipped crockery. Dented tin mugs. All were well cared for and loved.

Unfortunately, chipped edges were a hazard to my unsteady hands.

Crimson tainted the greasy water before I realized what occurred. I huffed, withdrawing my bloodied fingers from the cooling liquid. Azure gasped. I ignored the delicate noise, opting instead to pressure the minuscule wound.

"I have felled stone trolls with only a stick for a weapon, yet dishes make me bleed," I grumbled.

"Why don't we resume this later? We can sit at the table and talk while ye patch that."

Ah, there it is. A triumphant little smirk ticked my lip. I pulled myself along by the toes. With the skill of a thousand past experiences, I bound the cut and listened.

"I have two questions," Azure began.

"Oh joy," I mumbled, a wad of cloth between my teeth.

"About yer eye an' yer heritage."

My heritage? I froze. The latter, a fact many overlooked, oft evaded serious conversation. No one asked such questions. Only scholars, enthusiasts, and bigots. Azure suited none of the above. The spectral glow in her eyes shifted, pensive. I offered a slow nod. She resumed her interrogation, gentler.

"Please, pardon me bluntness but…what are ye?"

"A dwelf," I answered without hesitation or bravado. "An earf. Half-elven. Half-dwarven. I know no term for it."

"There is none."

Unused energy festered in the pit of my stomach. I stared at the notched table, yearning for some object or other to fidget. A knife. A scrap of bandage. Anything at all would suffice. Eventually, I stuck the leather strap from my bracer in my mouth and chewed. Deathly silence descended. The sort of silence that replaces Verve once the host passes into the world beyond.

"It explains the runes upon yer axe," Azure said at last.

I lifted my gaze. Leather squished and strained between my teeth. "How so?"

"They conflict. One is harsh and rigid. T' other is soft and curving. Neither are in Common."

"That certainly is astute of you," I mumbled.

"I have Sight."

The fiddle-strip dangled limply from my lips. Azure's eyes flashed a deeper blue. The blue of a summer sea. Her voice, ethereal and strong, matched the intensity of her gaze. I didn't answer.

"Ye have Spectral Gaze as well. Ye know what I see." Azure leaned across the table, voice near a whisper.

"Why?"

I let the leather drop from my mouth and grinned.

"Everyone has their secrets. This is one of mine."

"One of?" she repeated. My only answer was a wider smile. An inner strain pulled my heartstrings taut. Distant memories of my parents. Their love wholly felt yet hardly remembered. Haunted gray eyes and the helping hand they offered. The thoughts lent a tightness to my smile. A tension. Azure narrowed her eyes, seeking.

"Perhaps ye should dust while I finish the dishes."

"Agreed."

Azure fetched an odd contraption for me: a pole the length of my forearm with a plethora of rags bound to the end. I twirled the duster in my good hand. Dust fractals polluted the atmosphere about my arm. I coughed, reddening at my own foolishness.

Quietude elapsed as cleaning recommenced. Wisps of Verve fluttered through the cottage as Solasta and Bianca went about their respective chores. Their phantom wings flickered and sparkled alongside their emotions. Sunlight migrated from east to west. The day ebbed. Meals passed in joyful camaraderie.

When suppertime arrived, I sat in silence as the roses conversed. Simple food piled suspiciously high on my trencher. Was I honestly so ragged in appearance that they heaped my plate unnecessarily? Not that I would complain. More complaints meant less food.

"Do ye think it means anythin'? The magic I mean."

I froze, drinking in Solasta's comment as I slurped my willow bark tea. *What magic?* I wondered. Bianca waved the words aside.

"'Tis nothing. Right, Az?"

"Right." Azure took a tentative sip of her own tea. Our eyes met. Suspicion and curiosity clashed. My green eye saw through her calm demeanour. My gold eye saw through her ruse. No amount of self-restraint could hide the nervous flutter of her ephemeral wings.

"No," her firm eyes admonished.

"What magic?" I asked regardless. The blue rose stifled a huff.

"Nothin' much, Miss Finchley. Jist some odd currents Az saw in the Verve the other day. A blackness and all that."

"Oh?"

"Bianca!" Azure snipped, eyes aglow with ferocious blue light. "That's enough."

The pearlheaded faerie wilted. Her sharply pointed ears drooped, making me acutely aware of how squarish mine were in comparison.

Foolish girl. Don't be so vain! Yet their kindly Verve and radiant beauty made my skin crawl. Bianca's purity. Solasta's friendliness. The convoluted mystery that was Azure. Their magic bespoke everything I once wished to be. Everything I could no longer hope to become. No matter how many monsters I slayed, I was tainted. Beyond redemption. *Cursed.*

"Master's Mercy, what are those beauteous carvings?" Solasta burst. She seemed entirely unaware of the tension between her siblings. Master's Mercy indeed.

Solasta sprang from her seat and reverently stroked the floral pattern my father etched into the wood of my axe beneath the lacquer. The ornaments were rank with elven

Verve. Father's protective touch.

"Roses," I smiled. Nostalgia kindled a warmth in my stomach.

"Wot's a rose?"

"A flower. They grow all throughout my homeland."

"Where is that?" Bianca asked, ears perking up ever-so slightly.

"A long way from here," I laughed. "In the Copper Mountain Foothills to be precise. I have not sojourned there for many a year. Not since I lost the use of my legs."

"Ye mean t' say ye weren't always…?"

"No," I answered, saving Pearlhead the troublesome burden of labelling one such as I. I even managed a boisterous laugh for good measure. The hearty outburst incited gentle grins.

"No, a particularly vicious ogre snapped my legs in twain. Although…twain may be an understatement. An unfortunate side-effect of my profession."

I twisted my gnarled limbs to provide a better view. Malformed bones ground and twinged beneath my flesh. Lumps marked the impromptu 'joints' where bones severed and rejoined. Little did they know, constant bruises mottled my skin. Yet another side-effect.

The roses stared at my legs in unadulterated horror. Then again, I was accustomed to such reactions.

"May…may I speak plainly, miss?" Solasta breathed. The words seemed to lodge in her delicate throat. Even as I nodded for her to proceed, she hesitated. After much deliberation and grasping for words, she spoke.

"Why did ye not retire?"

I shrugged, leaning back in my wheeled chair. Instinctively, I went to rest my heels on the table. A stabbing pain bid me pause. I held back, annoyed. For alas, old habits were harder to slay than dragons. I should know.

"My skills belong to an incredibly specific criterion. I trained myself to track and kill evil, so kill I shall."

Solasta's golden skin paled to a faint yellow. Wide eyes peered from behind Bianca's unruly bangs. Azure remained placid. A rare talent among faeriekind.

"Death takes its toll on everyone. Especially on the one who survives. What price did you pay, Anonymous Finchley?" she inquired. My muscles tensed. Battle instincts fought decorum for supremacy.

They nearly won.

"What do you think?" I scoffed. To any normal being, my legs would be a blatant answer. Solasta and Bianca's subsequent discomfort proved as much. To one with Sight however...

Suffice it to say Azure straightened her already impeccable posture in silence.

The tension abated somewhat as Solasta pestered me for more floral information. What kinds of roses were there? What names did they have? Did they have names at all? What did they symbolize? Happily, I obliged. I poured forth what little botanical knowledge I possessed for her convenience.

Bianca's ears ceased their drooping. Each girl clasped their hands, as if clutching an imaginary bouquet. My Golden Gaze gave each their respective roses. Purity. Friendship. Mysterious intrigue. Three hues swirled about them in perfect harmony. They only grew brighter as I spoke. Catching a glimpse of my own Verve, I winced.

*"**Black,**" an unwelcome voice hissed. "**Your Verve reflects your soul, Anonymous. How can anyone love a hunter with a midnight soul? How can anyone love a monster?**"*

I ignored the obnoxious whisperings. My smile remained firmly in place. My voice stayed level. Why, then, did Azure's gaze narrow? Why did she watch me with such reservation and concern? These were understandable, albeit rude, but her most aggravating reaction of all was how she shuddered. She saw as I saw. She knew what I knew.

It sickened her. *I* sickened her.

Suddenly, I felt a crushing weight upon my chest and a tightness in my throat. The darkness seemed stronger than usual. The sheer brilliance of my companions augmented it. Azure saw through me. Let's simply say I didn't much care for having my disguises pierced.

Panicking, I feigned fatigue.

"Well, today has been lovely, my Roses, but I'm afraid I must retire." I yawned, stretching dramatically. "Might you have a guest room?"

"Of course," Bianca chirped. She sprang to her feet, aided by wings she did not realize she owned.

I wonder how shocked she'll be when they finally coalesce, I thought, shaking my head. Bianca led me across the room, then froze. Her ever-expressive ears twitched as she wrung her hands. I absent-mindedly stroked the hilt of my axe, waiting.

"I fear we do no' have a ground level room, Miss Finchley. We have a guest loft for ye but…" She spared a timid glance for my wheeled chair before studying the ground. A wry smile cracked my lip. Anticipation thrummed in my veins. The joy it sparked brightened the oppressive magic cloud. I gazed gleefully at the ladder and thought, *This. This I can do.*

"It's perfect," I insisted, rolling toward the rickety ladder. "My legs are useless. My arms are not."

With that, I shimmied out of my wheeled chair and scaled the splintering rungs. One arm after another, I climbed. Upward. I hauled myself ever upward. The strain was nigh unbearable yet invigorating. I pushed myself daily by arms and pulled by toes. Climbing was another matter. To climb was to rise above my limitations and conquer. Needless to say, I climbed often.

Once my elbows were over the loft's edge, I dragged myself across the floor via my forearms.

The loft was as quaint as the main floor. Wildflowers rested in a terracotta vase. Time-worn blankets neatly draped a thin pallet. One candle, cold and unlit, stood resolute at its bedside post.

Perfect, I concluded with a weary grin. Exciting as it was, climbing without legs took more strength than I cared to give.

"Goodnight, Roses," I called over the wooden precipice, more than a little breathless. However, the mixture of shock and pleasure in their expressions was well worth the exertion.

Beneath, the girls dispersed. They flittered about the kitchen, the candles waning as the moon waxed. Gold light sputtered and died. A chorus of gentle goodnights murmured through the loft adjacent to me. Silence followed, accompanied by silvery streams of light.

Silver, I thought with a shudder. The effervescent moonlight always felt too similar to grey for my liking. It resurrected memories best left dead. Nights alone and exposed under the moon's watchful glow. A grey gaze void of Verve yet irreparably kind. Grey steel sliced. Grey stone crushed. Silver Verve, once raw and beautiful, tainted by an ogre's malice until only black remained. Even with the shutters closed, silver light seeped into my darkness. It goaded me. *Taunted* me.

Yes, silver was far too akin to grey.

After a few fruitless hours abed, I sat up and growled, "No rest for the accursed."

So, silent as a shadow among trees, I slung my affects over my shoulder and descended. Splinters imbedded in my palms. The floorboards creaked tremendously beneath my wheels as I rolled into the kitchen. I half considered fleeing into the starry night to resume my hunt, yet guilt prompted me to stay. The Roses did not deserve such careless treatment as that. Wincing, I dug in my pack for an occupation. For work. Mindless toil. That was what I needed. I always stored one chore or another in preparation of sleepless nights. If I was not mistaken…

Aha! It just so happened that my mending had yet to be done. I lifted a mangled cloth jerkin from the deepest recesses of my bag. My golden eye gleamed with numb satisfaction.

I struck a match, the sudden warmth shocking me into wakefulness. The solitary flame kindled the wick of my once-bedside candle. The light was small, but strong. It would do nicely.

Stitching the worn fabric by candlelight, I allowed my

mind to dim. Sweet oblivion overtook my consciousness. Why think when thoughts harboured pain? Why dream when nightmares awaited?

In, out, and tighten. Thread swished through the dying garment in a final attempt to resuscitate it.

In. Out. In. Out. In. Out. Inhale. Exhale. Sew.

"Anonymous?"

I jumped, hand flying for my axe. Azure stood bleary-eyed before me. Unformed wings waved through the ladder she must have just descended. A tawny candle blazed in her grip. Wax dripped unnoticed onto her fingers. I massaged my temples and sighed.

"You should be asleep, Az," I muttered. Silver moonlight glinted off her skin. Couldn't the confounded stuff leave me in peace for once?

"As should ye."

"Can't sleep."

"Why is that?"

I shifted my wheeled chair, squinting in the wan candlelight. "Silver Maiden is watching."

Azure gazed through the open window to my left. She nodded, understanding. Yet how could she understand? Azure didn't have a beast turn her Verve inside-out. She need not worry about curses and omens. Above all, Azure was not a danger to her loved ones. She was not the harbinger of destruction I was. Yet she understood, and that disturbed me.

"Beast!" hissed the monstrous voice inside my head. **"Hideous beast!"** I flinched. Needle punctured skin as my hands began to shake. Red dripped onto the jerkin, mingling with the ancient bloodstains thereon. I muttered something unsavoury and rubbed away the ichor before it sank in too deep. Azure peered at the gore-mottled fabric, thoughtful.

"That blood does no' belong to ye," she mused.

"For the most part," I said, scrubbing. The stain lightened under my ministrations. My tremors lessened. With pinched lips and strained eyes, I resumed my sewing. Azure folded her hands on the table.

"What does the inscription say on yer axe?"

I sighed and bit back an agonizing wave of nostalgia. My own dwarven laughter mixing with the mirth of my parents. Fond farewells, those were. They shouted the inscription as I raced headlong into my destiny. Their final blessing. Why even read it? I knew the words by heart. I found myself caressing the carvings all the same.

"Mourn the dead,

"Cherish the living.

"Life be led,

"In courage and giving." I laughed sorrowfully. "They wrote it twice. Once in each script for good measure."

"They mist have truly loved ye."

"Still do," I said, giving my thread a solid jerk. "Leastwise they would if I bothered to visit."

"Why haven't ye?"

"They live in the mountains."

"And?"

I rapped my knuckles against the wheel well of my chair. Azure visibly deflated. Her eyes dimmed and her gaze drifted. Our candles danced in the throes of a gentle breeze. Their orange light bathed her contemplative face.

"What happened to yer Verve, Anon?" Azure whispered, masking a shiver. "It was no' always black. I can see that clear as I can see this candle."

Thread and jerkin went limp in my grasp as forbidden reminisces bombarded my mind. The foolish choices that led to a life in shambles. How my solitude became my downfall. It was a thing I preferred to forget.

Do not forget your weakness, I told myself, drawing a long breath.

"I used to say, 'Anonymous Finchley works alone.' That was my mantra. I used to see strength in solitude. Now, I see stupidity."

Azure leaned in, eyes agleam with…interest? No, with sympathy. It radiated from her quasi-formed wings in waves, urging me to continue. So, I did.

"There was an ogre," I sighed, "who slaughtered everyone in his path regardless of species or age. It was his daughter who enlisted my services: a stocky young ogress, kind and clumsy. Her father killed half her village, some of his own children included.

"I tracked that monster for days, following his blood-lust and hatred. His insanity. He waited for me at the trail's end, his mace rusted red and his clothing blood-spattered. We fought for hours. He snapped my legs. I hewed his arms. Eventually, I buried my axe in a death-blow. But it was too late. My legs were useless, twisted be-yond recognition or repair. And with his final breath he cursed me. 'My malice is now yours to bear. Fly from peace into despair.'"

I shuddered. The ogre's curse pounded against the door of my mind under the guise of a headache. Some-thing soothed it. A faint presence. I opened my eyes to see

Azure tensed as if to pounce. Her wings stretched forward, shielding me from the ogre's influence. The ogre. Master, I couldn't even bring myself to think his name! Azure nodded to me.

"Don't stop. Ye mist confront this," she whispered. Fingers wadding the doublet in my hands, I obeyed.

"I crawled through the underbrush, clawing my way toward the nearest settlement. Yet I tired. My body slowed. Blood loss weakened me as it poured from where bone punctured flesh. I laid in the brush and waited for death."

I wiped tears from my eyes. When had I started crying? Why couldn't I breathe right? It did not matter. My story mattered. That moment o'er two years ago *mattered*.

"Someone found me. A man, younger than I, with eyes so grey and lifeless I at first thought he was blind. He had no Verve. None. He stopped his journey for my sake and carried me to the town he left. He took me to an inn and paid for my care. Idiotically, I asked what happened to his Verve, his magic."

"What happened?"

"Claimed he never had any, that he almost gained some once but gave it away instead. 'Was it worth it?' I asked. He said, 'I don't know,' and left shortly thereafter. I never saw him again, and while I don't know his name, I will never forget his parting words: 'Verve isn't everything. Neither is mobility. Don't let either keep you down.' Sometimes I wonder if his words were worse than the ogre's or if I just don't understand him."

"Why is that?"

"If Verve is not everything and I define monsters by

their darkened Verve, what does that make me?"

"Anonymous, listen to me," Azure pleaded, taking my hand in hers. "The monsters ye killed were creatures of destruction. Their Verve reflected that. They chose death."

"So did I, Az. Face it, people are born for death. We come into this world to leave it."

Sound ceased, save for the crickets beyond the open window. Even Bianca and Solasta's faint snores stilled. They listened. I knew it. Azure knew it.

Let them listen. What does it matter if they do? Simple. It didn't. Such happenstances lost their meaning under the Silver Maiden's gaze. Even when wispy clouds dimmed her Sight.

Azure's wings closed tighter around me as my tears dried. They were safe, comforting. Azure squeezed my hand. Her mouth settled into a firm line. Immovable. Placid. Wise. These were Azure and, despite all her previous glares, I let myself fall under her sway.

"Anon," she said. Her voice was soft, firm as the sand beneath the sea, "a candle is not lit for the sake of burning out. It is lit to give light to the world around it. It is the same with life."

"No wonder some people set fire to the world. They step out of bounds then watch it burn," I scoffed, pulling my hand away. A foolish gesture. Especially considering I was ensconced by her rapidly solidifying wings. I tried to care and failed.

"Ye are *no'* a monster as ye think. Ye are a sign, and I apologize for holdin' that against ye."

Azure shifted. Her wings were nearly visible to my

green eye. Incandescent glyphs spread across her cheeks and ears. Light brushstrokes composed the lettering: faerie script. Guilt festered beneath them in an ice-blue blush. Her skin, once pinkish and pale, transitioned to a heavenly cobalt blue.

Her sisters gasped, peeking over the loft's edge. Their own transformations had yet to begin.

Azure took my hand once more.

"I grew up knowing that one day we would leave our cottage t' reside elsewhere. Some place from which we shall grant gifts to those who seek them and wishes to those beyond natural aid. As dearly as I love our home, faeries are not static beings. We are born to bless. Yer coming…it is the impetus."

"Meaning?"

"Meaning we can free ye from this curse."

My mind screeched to a halt. An avalanche of thought followed. It tumbled and crashed in an incomprehensible muddle. Words clogged my throat. My omnipresent thundercloud, the voice that stole my sleep at night, could she truly banish it? An intoxicating blend of hope and despair sprung to life within me.

Could I be free of my curse?

"H-how is—how is that possible?" I finally stammered. "What must I do?"

"Make a trade," Azure answered. Solasta and Bianca slid down their ladder, nightgowns rumpled by sleep.

"A trade?" I pressed.

"Something of value for a gift beyond price."

I shook my head and sighed. I hadn't owned anything of value since…

Wait.

I unhitched the axe from my belt and proffered it to the faerie. The blade gleamed under the moon's silver gaze. The protective inscription felt accusative beneath my grip. Trade my axe, my livelihood and intended family heirloom, to some girls I barely knew?

"Will this do?" I asked, not giving myself a chance to reconsider.

Azure took the battle-axe in her hands, reverent. She smiled up at her sisters. The half-faeries stepped forward. Each laid a hand on the axe haft, gazing down at Azure in expectance. I watched them through my green eye as their inner radiance burst forth.

Solasta's golden skin outshone the sun, infecting her hair and eyes all at once. Bianca paled to shame the stars as her eyes blanched. She went white beyond natural bounds yet seemed anything other than sickly. Between them, Azure morphed to match her Spectral Gaze: blue. Three hues combined. Three roses infused my axe, devouring it in a shower of splinters and steel.

My mind blanked. Instinctively, I shielded my eyes. Gentle pulses thrummed over me. Enraged screams faded into nothingness within the dregs of my soul. Blackness abated. Freedom prevailed. A sweet melody resounded in my heart. Kind, and lovely, and free. I opened my eyes.

Three divinities stood around the table. They floated above the debris on vibrant pinions. My axe laid scattered upon the cottage floor. Tentatively, I viewed my hands, Golden Gaze intact.

My curse was gone.

"I don't..." A lump lodged in my throat, obstructing

my thanks. "I don't know what to say other than 'thank you.'"

"Say nothing more. 'Thank ye' is more than enough," Azure said, bowing her sapphire head.

"Sol?" Bianca breathed. She gazed down at her blanched hands in disbelief.

"Yes?"

"Are we flyin'?"

"I believe we are," Solasta laughed. She twirled midair, relishing her weightlessness. Their brilliant magic illuminated the dwelling. Shadows fled. Only light persisted in the quaint cottage.

Azure squeezed my hand one last time. She smiled through her tears. Blue tresses brushed my shoulder as she pressed her forehead against my own. Warm tears bathed my cheeks. Azure's tears.

"Thank ye for yer help. May we meet again."

Without another word, Azure took her sisters by the hand and led them through the open window. They flew far into the night. Higher and farther than I ever could have imagined. For all I knew, they could have transcended the sky. I watched until the girls shrank like stars into the distance. Formless yet beautiful.

I was free.

The Silver Maiden and I sat alone. For once, I didn't mind the company.

The Merrow Child

The Merrow Child

I was drowning.

I could feel the water pouring into my lungs as the ship's debris hauled me into the depths. The sea felt cold. Deathly cold as it closed in around me.

Drowsiness fogged my mind. The pain in my chest dulled. I was dying and powerless to stop it. Tangled ropes dug into my ankle, tying me to the very cannon I swore to maintain. I could still catch glimpses of the fiery blasts above. Had anyone seen me fall? Would they care?

So…tired…

I closed my eyes. The eddying current swirled about me. Predatory fins brushed my cheek, cutting it. Blood tinged the water crimson. An aquatic chirp coaxed me toward consciousness. Icy hands cradled my face. My vision wavered and blurred. My eyes drifted shut, unable to register what I had seen. A girl? A fish? Perhaps both.

Something clawed at my foot. I tried to scream. Nothing came. Neither sound nor bubbles penetrated the deepness, for I had no air left to surrender. Only my life remained. To that I clung.

Claws dug into the raw flesh. I thrashed, gazing down at my snared foot in desperation. As my mind finally went black, a merrow slashed the rope that bound my ankle. I felt myself being lifted and knew no more.

* * *

"Breathe, human! *Breathe!*" A frantic, trilling voice pleaded. The girl chirred, pounding my back with a webbed fist. The sea itself tore through my chest, scraping its way out. Water spewed from my mouth. It leaked from my lungs and onto…land? No, a rock. Cannons fired in the distance, easily drowned by my hacking coughs. The girl chirped in relief. Bluish arms cradled me. A gentle, aquatic lullaby soothed my soul as the singer rubbed circles between my shoulder blades.

We remained that way for ages. She sang in a language as majestic as the waves. I vomited water until my aching lungs adjusted to the air. Bracing myself, I dared to look up at my rescuer.

Seaweed-green hair framed her cerulean face. She smiled, flaunting razor-sharp teeth. Eyes as black as a midnight sea stared down at me. Cold yet comfortable. Terrifying yet gentle. A merrow, just as my mother used to tell me stories about. A battle raged on in the distance, the orange light illuminating the merrow's face.

"Don't you go chasing after merrows, lad," Mum always said. *"They are flighty things and not overfond of humans. Best to keep your distance."*

"Why…" I never had a chance to finish. Even the slightest effort to talk incited a coughing fit so ragged I ceased to breathe. The merrow pet and soothed me as one would a cat until my hacking subsided.

"Shh…" she chittered, voice echoing oddly. "Don't speak. You had a rough go of it, lad. Rest now."

"My…ship…"

The merrow stared into the distance. The blacks of her eyes narrowed into slits, revealing sea green irises. She bared her shark-like teeth as her ears, or rather fins, drooped.

"Pirates. You fell over the side just before they boarded," she hissed.

Boarded?! I heaved upward. My vision swam and my mind whirled. Nausea churned in the depths of my stomach. A forceful, finned hand shoved me back down.

"There's nothing you can do, lad. It's over."

"My captain…my crew…my family…"

"I'm sorry. You poor bairn. Don't you worry, lad. I shall take good care of you."

Despite myself, despite all the times I told myself men do not cry, I sobbed. My body heaved. The pain of the drowning burned fresh in my lungs. The merrow hugged me against her chest. A tunic woven of seaweed and pearls squelched beneath my trembling grip. My head pounded. My chest hurt. My heart *ached.* Everyone I knew and loved was on that ship. They were as good as dead.

The merrow gently shushed me, resuming her song.

The words rolled off her tongue and bounced off the lapping waves. Her eyes trailed the horizon. After a while, she gazed at the rising stars.

"What am I going to tell Alessia?" she murmured. In an attempt to speak, I coughed up more seawater. The salty bile burned its way through my lungs and out my throat. It spewed onto my rescuer's chest. If the merrow hadn't been drenched already, I would have felt remorse over the state of her shirt.

"Poor human. What do they call you? I am Chika."

"Dec…lan…" I managed between gasps.

"Declan," Chika chirred. "I need you to put this pearl in your mouth."

"Wha—what?"

Chika tore a pearl from her tunic and offered it to me. The white orb glistened in the eventide sun.

"So long as it is in your mouth, you can breathe under the waves. Do not speak, lest it fall out. And don't swallow, for I might want it back. Can you do this for me?"

Weakly, I nodded.

Before I could comment further, Chika shoved the pearl into my mouth and dragged me into the watery depths. It took all my restraint not to scream. The waves closed above our heads. Chika kept a firm grip on my wrist, propelling us downward with each stroke of her majestic tail. Surprisingly, the water flowed through my lungs like air. It was as if my entire respiratory system shifted to accommodate the bead.

The pearl sat awkwardly inside my mouth. It rolled and prodded yet my breath streamed around it. The calcium lump sank into my tongue.

Is this how it feels to be a clam? I wondered.

Chika dragged me deeper. Away from land. Away from sunset and starlight. All I could see was her bioluminescent body as we continued to descend. And descend. And descend.

Her scales and skin shone with an inner radiance. Surrounded by deepness itself, I realized how truly enormous Chika was. She dwarfed me. If I included her tail, she was nearly twice my length. Muscles that put most swimmers to shame formed her arms and undoubtably her torso. Catching my gaze, Chika giggled and hauled me further into the blackness.

She wouldn't save you just to drown you. She wouldn't save you just to drown you, I thought to myself as I shut my eyes against the current.

The water chilled the deeper she dove. No sunlight dared breach the all-encompassing waves. Soft, chittering voices filled the ocean beneath. Currents and eddies flowed about me. They comforted me; coaxed my eyes open.

In that moment, I saw a paradise.

Luminescence surged through the city below as surely as wind washed over cities above. Seashells tall as brigantines lined the ocean floor in haphazard arcs. Whalebone pavilions, grottos, and stone mounds dotted the subaqueous city. Merrows and fish swam through sunken ships repurposed into homes. The pearl nearly dropped from my mouth as I gasped.

Chika dragged me toward a half-rotten treasure galleon. Florescent stones studded the hull. A host of aquatic plants sprang from the waterlogged wood. Seashell garlands hung over an ornate gap in the ship's side. Merrows waited on either side of the entrance, their spears and shields erect. Their tails were long and muscular. Dark and sharklike, their fins quivered constantly. The mermen eyed Chika with fond suspicion.

"What do you have this time, Chika?" one of the merrows sighed. I jolted as I instinctively ducked behind my mermaid guardian.

The guards spoke in their musical language, yet I understood them. I comprehended every word.

What in Jarrel's name caused that? I wondered, clinging to Chika's tunic. Bubbles swirled as Chika hauled me to the forefront. She held me up appraisingly, grinning with her razor teeth.

"Isn't he adorable?" she trilled. Warmth crept into my cheeks. If embarrassment were lethal, I would have been long dead. The merrow guards groaned.

"Another pet, Chika?" said the second guard. Chika turned up an indignant, scaly nose.

"I'll have you know he is a human, not some orphaned fish I snuck into the palace."

"I see…"

The first guard massaged his forehead, expression caught between a grimace and a grin.

"Queen Alessia will be displeased. You know this."

Chika's fins bristled. A growling huff, as feline as it was aquatic, rumbled in her throat. It sounded protective. Like a mother sea lion laying claim to her cubs. A sense of nervous dread knotted itself in my stomach. With Chika's defensive claws curled about my forearms, I wondered if I would ever see the sky again. Would the merrows let me?

"You know my tactics well enough, Seth, to understand a simple 'no' won't daunt me," my rescuer replied. She swam past the guards without resistance. The mermen cast curious looks at her cargo, tilting their blue-tinted heads. I covered my face with one hand and clung to Chika with the other. Having heavily armed merrows stare into my soul unsettled me. Especially when said merrows had pure black eyes and protruding incisors.

Seaweed and pearl garlands decked the ship's interior. Iridescent stones lined the walls. Very little of the inner levels remained and what did was molding and rotten. Seashell ornaments and multihued crystals hung from the underside of the deck in a glittering array. Merrows swam through the repurposed wreckage. Their tails, fins, and spines shone in the deep darkness, revealing their inner majesty. Each paused to stare. Some even dared follow Chika on her winding trajectory. A particularly curious merman, a mere boy by his people's standards, kept himself within arm's reach at all times. His pure turquoise eyes glimmered with interest. My face glowed with a more reserved light as the attention sent it blazing.

Chika plunged into the depths of the hull. I squinted through the waters until her destination revealed itself to my dim sight.

A throne of shells, gemstones, clams, and pearls rested upon a rock that pierced the ship's underbelly. Upon that throne perched a merrow of unparalleled regality. Hair whiter than sea foam swirled placidly in the water about her head, adorned by a mauve coral crown. Her face was grim, green, and wrinkled as a riled sea. Silver eyes shone from beneath ebony eyelashes. I suddenly had the insatiable desire to bow. Unfortunately, Chika decided to obscure me at that precise moment.

The merqueen stiffened, drawing a deep breath through her gills.

"Chika?" she demanded. "What do you have behind your back?"

I could practically *feel* Chika's grin. The merrow gave a bubbly chittering noise, tail swishing methodically.

"You see, your majesty, I was swimming near the surface to watch the fight, as you do—"

"I don't."

"—and something fell overboard. I went to investigate and well…"

The underwater world blurred as Chika held her find up to the merqueen: me. Regal merrow stared down awed human. Once again, my face burned a deep crimson.

"Look at him!" Chika implored. "How can you say no to that face?"

"No." The merqueen's eyes narrowed as her ear-fins flattened against the sides of her head. Bashful, I glanced up at Chika. The mermaiden's eyes swelled impossibly large. She pouted, flaunting her incisors.

"Please? I'll take good care of him, I promise."

How in Zander can I understand them? I wondered once again. Taking a long breath, I experimentally popped the pearl out of my mouth. An entire ocean's weight pressed in on me. Air became a distant memory as I stopped breathing altogether. The merrow language faded into a senseless muddle of trills and chittering. I shoved the pearl between my teeth before I suffocated.

"—cannot allow it! Humans do not belong under the

sea," the merqueen argued, her wrinkled brow furrowing into a thousand miniature trenches. My heart sank. Chika's, evidently, did not.

"Can we make him a merrow then?" she pleaded. "I know how."

Every frequency of warning blared in my mind. *Me? A merrow? How? Why? No. A thousand times no!* My thoughts skittered to a halt as the turquoise-eyed merrow swam gingerly up to Chika.

"Can I…can I pet him?" the boy asked.

"Sure!"

This is humiliating, I inwardly grumbled as the adolescent merrow stroked my waterlogged tresses. I waited in silence as the merchild ran his overlong fingernails through the finest substance known to merrow-kind: human hair.

"His hair is so soft! Oh, Alessia, can't she keep him?"

Chika turned to the merqueen, her posture beyond hopeful. "Please, Mama?"

Queen Alessia sighed. She pinched the bridge of her nose until red indents marred where nail met skin. The expression of a surreptitiously lenient mother contorted her elegant features.

"Fine, but *only* if you transform him and *only* if you keep him out of trouble. Am I clear?"

"Thank you! Come on, Declan. This way. My sisters are going to love you," Chika squealed.

"*After* I have a word with the lad," the merqueen added. Her severe tone allowed no room for argument.

Chika winced, sighing to herself. With a whispered prayer, she surrendered me to her mother's care.

"Fear not, Declan. Her majesty is kinder than she appears."

I nodded to Chika, hoping her encouragement proved truthful. She smiled. Her shark teeth glimmered in the surrounding phosphorescence as her inner radiance shone forth.

An imposing guard swam from the gathered throng I caused. The merrow was easily twice my height, thrice my width, and beyond stunning in the sheer power of her physiology. She propelled herself behind Queen Alessia's throne and drew back a swath of shell-studded garlands. Beyond them laid a dark room. An audience chamber.

Blue stones littered the floor within, casting barely enough luminescence for a human to see by. Alessia waved me inside. Drawing a watery breath, I obeyed.

Once the seaweed veil fell into place behind us, Alessia seized my arm. I jolted but resisted the urge to scream. Her black talons wavered on the ridge between vigilant and possessive, much like her daughter. She led me through the dimly lit chamber to a lone boulder.

"Have a seat, human," she ordered. I did as commanded, although the thick hydrosphere made keeping still rather difficult. The merqueen floated in front of me, regal as she was calm.

"I will ask you a series of questions and you will answer them regardless of the pearl in your mouth. If anything goes amiss, I shall help you. Do you understand?"

"Yes," I replied, cradling the orb in my cheek.

"Good." Alessia fixed her gaze upon me, intent. "Do you wish to become a merrow?"

"No."

"Why not?"

"I have a life on land."

"Do you now?" she probed, somewhat doubtful. I clenched my teeth to hold any irreverent remarks at bay. The rope burn and slashes upon my ankle throbbed in remembrance. The cut upon my cheek stung. I clearly recalled the terror, the utter hopelessness I felt as debris hauled me into the depths of the West Sea. Debris from my ship.

My life was gone.

"Not anymore," I answered.

"Oh?"

"That life is over."

"Then why do you cling to your humanity? What hope is there in those legs of yours?"

Alessia's silver eyes glimmered like moonlight upon a windswept sea. They questioned. Challenged. A chill sunk into my bones as I drew another saltwater breath.

"Why are you asking me this?" I whispered. The merqueen's fins quivered.

"To see if you know what you want."

"I want to go home."

"Do you?" she pressed. My lungs constricted despite my pearl. A lump lodged in my throat, obstructing further speech for a time. I shook my head. A deep blush crept into my cheeks at my error. Alessia placed a webbed hand upon my shoulder. Green luminosity brightened the room as she willed her body to shine.

"What do you want?" she prompted.

"My family," I managed, choking upon unshed tears. The merqueen nodded.

"Do they live?"

"I don't know."

Queen Alessia extended her other hand to cup my cheek. I leaned into her touch, my eyes drifting closed as I remembered the hundreds of times Mum did the same. Only the merqueen was not my mother. Far from it. Mum was small, gentle, and easily missed in a crowd. Alessia was a twelve-foot merrow that made even the tallest of men feel small when compared to her royal bulk.

"The decision is yours, child. Chika will guide you through the process if you wish to proceed. If not..." Alessia paused, offering a reserved smile. "I wish you peace and good fortune on your journeys to come."

She slipped through the garland door with all the elegance befitted her station. I followed. A cobalt blur greeted me behind the throne. Chika clasped my hands in hers, trilling excitedly.

"Her majesty told me you would decide in a moment. Come this way."

The ecstatic merrow dragged me into the upper reaches of the ship. Currents, ornaments, and debris rushed past. The casual bioluminescence shocked my senses. I had always expected the ocean to be cold and dark. Austere even. Yet as Chika led me through the darkness, I saw light, warmth, and life. A fresh world beyond my wildest imagining awaited with open arms. Meanwhile...

Meanwhile my family is under attack. They're in trouble and I'm off galivanting with merfolk. The realization settled like a cannonball in my stomach. When I closed my eyes, I could still feel the tremors. The sensations of the deck splintering beneath my feet. Of sinking downward into a cold, dark abyss.

High-pitched trills startled me from my reverie. A cluster of elaborately dressed mermaids streaked toward me. One hung back, stern and commanding like her mother.

"Another pet, Chika?" she droned.

"Not a pet, a *friend*. See?"

Chika's sister saw but remained unfazed. An expression of sheer boredom encompassed her demeanour. Her pod of siblings, however, rushed upon me, enthralled. One girl plucked a strand of shell-encrusted seaweed from the wall and wove it into a play crown. I sighed, allowing her to place the ornamentation on my head. The mermaid giggled to herself. Her sharklike smile reflected the oscillating lights.

The more reserved princess glared at me through charcoal eyes. Displeased was an understatement. Chika's older sister was indignant from the tip of her tail to the ends of her coiled hair. The other merrows fawned over their new prize. Some even dared to pet me. Chika herself disappeared. I suffered it all with a deep blush, unable to speak and unwilling to move.

"Honestly, girls, you're going to smother him," the reserved merrow scoffed. A young coral-tinted mermaid huffed back.

"He's fine, Valora."

"Oh really? Have you asked him?" Valora trilled. The princesses turned to me. In that singularly awkward moment, I found I could not meet their eyes. A hush fell over the crowded waters. An inexplicable shiver consumed me. I hugged myself in a vain attempt to ward off the sudden chill. I glanced bashfully toward Valora, both grateful and frightened.

Chika glided into the chamber, a white conch shell in her hands. Bright, oily liquid wavered within the alabaster confines. Confusion pinched her cerulean skin. She glanced at Valora, tilting her head in question.

"Everyone out except Chika," Valora ordered, shooing her sisters toward the exit. Some groaned. Most obeyed their senior in grim silence. The curtain closed behind the merrows, leaving Chika and I alone. Chika stared at me for a long moment before daring to speak.

"Is something wrong, Declan?" She fiddled with the conch shell. The red liquid sloshed inside, separate from the water around it. Cautiously, I set the pearl between my teeth.

"My family," I stated simply. To say anything more threatened to dislodge the cork on my emotions. Chika's fins quivered in understanding. The pearl slipped, rolling onto my tongue as I clamped my mouth shut. Hesitant, Chika pressed the conch shell into my unsteady hands. Gentle and musing, she met my eyes and smiled.

"You don't have to drink it, Declan. If you decide not to, knock twice on the wall and I'll find you a port to make your home in. But if you want to be a merrow, drink. Whatever you decide, I know you'll always be one of us at heart and that is enough for me. You are truly one with the sea. I can feel it."

Chika whisked out of the chamber. Her tail caught on the curtain, revealing a dozen eavesdropping princesses on the other side. Eager aquatic faces peeked through sea-weed and pearls. Valora shoved them aside, providing me a much-needed moment of privacy.

I floated aimlessly in the sunken ship, pondering. My whole life above the surface laid in shambles. My livelihood as a sailor was sinking to the ocean floor even as I drifted there. Pirates ravaged the waters I once called home. They held my parents, sister, and crewmates captive.

If they are alive at all…

As a human, I could do nothing. No one man could upend an entire corsair crew. Less so a man who had barely reached adulthood. As a merrow however…

The pirates would never see it coming. The element of surprise might prevail. That, and if the oldest Zandarian myths were true, the sea itself would be at my beck and call. A faint hopefulness thrummed in my chest at the thought.

But…could I really sacrifice my identity, my humanity, for such a feeble hope? My family and friends could be dead for all I knew. I might trade my race for nothing. Trust in a potentially false hope or live on in guilt. Neither option appealed to me. I glanced from my idle legs to the door.

Before I could hesitate a moment longer, I spat the pearl and downed the red liquid in a single gulp.

My chest spasmed. My bones rearranged. Skin split to form gills along my neck and hips. Clothing tore and drifted away. My body morphed, changing in an agonizing betrayal against nature. I glanced downward only to see a tail and fins where legs should have been. I gasped. Water rushed in my mouth and out my gills. The strange sensation caused me to clutch my throat in alarm. Frantic, I found myself searching for a mirror.

There! I swam awkwardly toward the polished looking glass. My cumbersome tail knocked over several fixtures along the way. In the mirror, I saw the strangest merrow in existence.

My face stayed the same throughout the transformation. Rounded ears instead of fins, blunt teeth, soft hair. Everything from my shoulders upward appeared inherently human. Even my torso remained nigh unchanged. Yet the difference was unmistakeable. Fins bedecked my arms at the elbow and sprouted from my hips. A striking maroon tail blended into my swarthy skin. Gills sliced my flesh as surely as knife wounds.

I folded my finned arms over my exposed chest and blushed to match my tail. Regardless, I eased the seashell curtain open. The princesses awaited in tense silence inside some semblance of a hallway. Chika surged forward. She grasped my shaking hands and grinned.

Every merrow save the youngest continued to dwarf me. Despite my twenty years, I appeared a child in comparison.

"I want to save them," I said.

"Who, dearie?" one of the princesses asked. A young thing not much larger than myself. Her black eyes glimmered with curiosity and awe.

"My family. I don't want to let the pirates take them. Not today. Not *ever.*"

Chika clutched me tighter, terror in her eyes. "Declan, *love,* I know your heart is in the right place, but these are pirates. You've only had your fins for a minute. Less than!"

"And if you were me, Chika? If someone took your

family and you possessed the slightest chance of stopping them, would you not at least try?"

No one dared to answer me. Only currents stirred. A few of the merwomen blocked the exits. They glanced from one sister to the next. Quiet tension leached into the waters as the impasse stood. I sighed but no bubbles appeared.

"I'm not asking for support. I am asking permission."

I shuddered, trembling as I fought to conceal my tears. What did they matter under the ocean? The waters devoured them as it devoured all things that trespassed within her. Desperation clawed at my heart. Forbidden images flared before my mind's eye. My family in trouble. My crew in pain. Atrocities waited to be committed a few short leagues above me. I needed, physically *needed*, to stop them.

"Chika, I am begging you, let me go. I'll do whatever you ask. If you want, I will stay forever and ever with you here, but please, *please* let me save them!"

Chika rested her webbed hands upon my shoulders. She pressed her forehead against my own. A mournful trill rumbled in her throat, sending her gills quivering.

"Go with my blessing," she whispered.

I streaked past the merrows and through a hole in the ceiling without hesitation. The city's luminescence gave way to darkness. As the natural gloom pressed in, my newfound scales lit the way. A halo of vermillion light protected me.

Neither shark nor fish risked crossing paths with a merrow on a mission.

As the waning sunlight finally filtered through the waters, I shot up through the surface. I broke free, gasping reflexively. A lone ship retreated in the distance. The pirate brigantine.

A medley of emotions played through my heart. Terror. Excitement. Joy. Pain. Everything I hoped for and feared skidded across the horizon. A horizon that laid well within a merrow's reach. My reach. Around me, dozens of merrows surfaced. Chika, Alessia, Valora. Even the turquoise-eyed youth joined their ranks.

From their midst, Queen Alessia nodded to me. A wordless covenant, for no words were needed. Once a merrow, always a merrow. That made me part of their family. A family that protected one another and attacked together.

The merrows and I skimmed across the waters as one. Waning sunlight glinted off the waves in shimmering beams. The pirate ship drifted lazily along some ambiguous course. Rough laughter tainted the wind. Blood boiled in my veins, fuelled by an amount of anger I seldom allowed myself to feel. I unleashed it, pouring all my strength into reaching the ship before things could go further amiss.

Chika wove between the other merfolk, manoeuvring her way closer to me. She eyed the schooner warily, fins all aquiver.

"Declan? Is there a plan?" she asked, her voice barely audible above the roaring waves. Only the slightest hint of concern tainted the mermaiden's tone. The rest she hid beneath an enviable veneer of composure.

"Nope."

"You should have a plan."

"I'm open to suggestions."

The merrow trilled thoughtfully. Her black eyes glinted, reflecting the churning waves.

"We could sink it," she said.

"That might kill everyone on board!"

"Unless we turned them into merrows."

"You can't solve all your problems by turning humans into merrows, Chika."

"A mere suggestion. Nothing more." Despite her flippant tone, Chika appeared half-heartedly offended. I could amend that later. At the moment, I had more pressing matters to attend to. The life and death sort.

Gears and pulleys jolted in my mind. I forced them to toil and spin until the answers formulated. Water parted before my fins. It flew up to splash my unguarded face. The ship drew nearer as the solution fled further. I needed a plan. Something simple. Something harsh. Something—

"Superstition!" I burst. Chika nearly foundered in surprise. "Pirates are notorious for their superstition!"

A myriad of merrows looked at me as if I had gone insane. Chika, however, literally glowed in excitement. Her eyes sparkled like the twilit sky above. The brightest stars reflected in the water alongside the luminescent merfolk.

And the pirates called themselves the terror of the four seas. Ha! They had yet to meet the true wave masters of Jarrel's province. Blood, loyalty, war. The merrows lived and died these traits under the sea as surely as the humans did above. Except the pirates weren't the ones with fangs.

"We play it safe," I ordered. "We prey on their superstition and demand they hand all their prisoners over to us."

"Like a sacrifice?" Valora asked. For once, her tone lacked any condescension whatsoever.

"More or less."

Chika grinned. Her teeth shone in the aura of her own luminosity "I hope you know how to act."

Oh Runa, she's going to enjoy this isn't she? I thought with a shake of my head.

The brigantine loomed closer on the horizon. My torso and tail ached. Their glow dulled to an almost painful shade of crimson as I pushed beyond my physical boundaries. I pointedly ignored the concern in Chika's eyes. I could rest another time. When my family was safe, I would sink into the watery depths and absorb the salted hydrosphere. I could calm down then.

We slowed to a silent crawl as we neared the barnacled hull. Queen Alessia lifted herself onto the tips of her tail to eavesdrop. Her mouth compressed into a somber line.

"Well?" I asked as she descended.

"You must have one incredible plan, child. They are hopeless otherwise."

My blood went colder than the ocean. The colour drained from my scales. A dim, grayish cast surged up my tail and into my skin. Chika jerked away, surprised. Valora merely blinked. I ran my hands through my waterlogged hair and *breathed*.

"Alright," I whispered. "Do. Not. Panic. We can fix this. Just think."

The merrows went silent. The lapping waves nearly drowned out the boisterous seamen above. Their laughter goaded me. Every curse and jeer burned within my chest. The colour returned to my body in a rush. Anger and inspiration tainted my entire being red. I whirled toward Alessia, nearly keeling over at the sudden motion.

"Can merrows create pillars of water as the stories say?"

The merqueen nodded. Her sage eyes reflected my own thoughts. I pointed toward the ship's deck, allowing myself a devious grin. Not a day gone by, yet Chika had already infected me.

"Raise me on a pillar. I know what to do."

Alessia complied. Water swelled about my waist, holding me fast. I shot hundreds of feet into the air. The pillar obscured my tail perfectly. Currents and eddies secured me to the column like ropes. I ascended above the deck, only stopping when I towered over pirate and prisoner alike. With all my might, I channelled my luminescence to capture their attention.

Mum was the first to notice. She huddled next to Dad, looking to the heavens for aid. Instead of the provincial Defendants or The Master, she saw me. Her son. A beacon of ruby light.

She screamed.

I turned my eyes away, focusing on the corsairs. The savage thieves stared skyward in horror. Red radiance shone through my eyes as I vented my fury through them. For all I knew, I looked like Jarrel in the legends during the Severing War. Fierce, enraged, and blood red.

"You killed me," I growled. I bled as much accusation into my tone as possible. Crimson brilliance shone forth from my skin. My light strengthened, illuminating the entire ship. The pirates scampered across the deck, terrified. They screamed oaths and omens as they ran. Perfect.

"You killed me and took my family. I want them back. Give them to the sea."

"Oh, great spectre," the captain ventured, "we meant no disrespect. We merely——"

"*DISRESPECT?!* You shot me down like an animal and you claim you 'meant no disrespect?' I could kill all of you this instant. Instead, I ask for a simple favour. Give. My family. Back. Every last crew member."

The pirates did not argue twice. They dragged my crew toward the plank. The victims shrieked. Some called out to me, fearful. I steeled myself, forcing my expression to remain impassive.

Chika, I hope you're ready to catch some more humans.

"Declan, you idiot!" my sister hollered. "What the depths has gotten into you?!"

The captain threw her overboard before she could utter another syllable. The turquoise-eyed merrow leapt from the waters and caught her midair. Once secure in the sea, he promptly began to stroke Rhea's hair. My sister stared toward me in mute confusion. It took all my self-control not to smile. I nodded to the buccaneers, ordering them to proceed.

One by one, my crew members plunged into the sea. One by one, the merrows caught them. Each scream shot through my heart like an arrow. Every splash made me glance toward the aquatic throng below. As the last person stepped off the plank, the corsair captain turned hopeful eyes upon me.

You thought you were a fearsome lord of the seas, but you are no more than a superstitious worm. Pathetic, I thought. Rather than vent such sentiments audibly, I chose something less personal and more ominous.

"Turn from your heinous ways or be destroyed. This is your only warning."

Alessia dissolved the pillar. I plunged soundlessly into the waves. Blue hands grabbed hold of me before I could even resurface. Chika dragged me against the hull in a spine-crushing hug. She trilled a manic giggle.

"Well done, Dec! You had every last one of those sea slugs grovelling at your fins."

I responded with an incoherent rumble of nervous laughter. A human hand gripped my shoulder.

"Declan," Rhea said sternly. "Where in Jarrel's name are your legs?"

I looked from my tail to Rhea then shrugged. "Nowhere, and please stop swearing by our ancestor."

"Why? Everyone else does it. Jarrel wasn't even our direct predecessor. His younger brother was."

"A minor detail."

"Um, Declan? I hate to interrupt this wonderful reunion but…" Chika cast her eyes upward. Pirates leaned over the bulwark, watching us with saucer-sized eyes. Accusative shouts rattled the night air. "They appear to be onto us. What now?"

A stuttering *tha-thump* replaced my regular heartbeat. Palpitations wracked my chest and set my gills quivering. I forced myself into a state of calm, letting my subdued breathing do the work. Gradually, a plan congealed in my mind. An outline formed. The fuzzy details could be ignored at present. I whirled on my new fins, unsteady at best, to face merrows and humans alike.

"Valora, you and your sisters take the crew ashore. I

trust you know a safe place to put them?"

"Do I ever." Valora smirked, her razor teeth a wonderfully gruesome sight.

"As for the rest of you, we run the ship aground and let the island authorities take over from there."

Valora skimmed away, bearing my sister Rhea with her. The indignant sailor cursed and thrashed at the sudden motion.

Grim enthusiasm settled over the waters. Shouts shattered the night's growing tranquility. I refused to let them shatter my resolve as well. I raised my hands above my head, reaching out to the water with every iota of Verve in my body. The waves responded, cheerful. Eager to serve.

I shoved the responsive waters against the brigantine's hull. Alessia did the same. The remaining merrows followed our lead, creating a flash flood upon the sea itself. Boards creaked and groaned. The sails fluttered violently as they were forced opposite the wind. Masts snapped under the pressure. The brigantine surged across the sea, caught in the throes of our impromptu current.

Ship met shore with a thunderous crash. Queen Alessia smiled.

"Well done, young one," she said. "Perhaps I judged you too quickly."

Our pod swam to Valora's chosen shore in silence. Solemnity hung over us. A level of quietude split only by the lapping waves. Darkness, split only by our glow. The queen kept her hand on my spine to guide me. Her webbed fingers trembled, chilled by the night air.

Starlight punctured the sky, accompanied by a brilliant crescent moon. The rocky shoals glimmered. Gulls and basilisks called to one another through the gathering mist. Eager waves crashed against the rocks, coating them in a layer of slick sea foam.

Chika greeted me amid the shallow waters. Our tails stirred the pebbles beneath. Upon the shore, a crowd of humans waited. Their tattered clothing, slumped postures, and glazed eyes bespoke the exhaustion they surely felt. Rhea pulled our parents aside. Her mouth opened and closed at a frightening pace as she scrambled to explain something or other. She kept a firm hand on each of their shoulders, bracing them. For what?

Mum's gaze landed on me. She jolted away, shocked as she was terrified. Dad's eyes drifted to my luminescent tail and fins.

Oh, I realized. *They didn't know.*

Dad was the first, and only, to recover. He sprinted across the shifting stones, his motions frantic and weary. Before I could even blink, he leapt into the sea and caught me in his arms. Hitching sobs wracked his body. His hand combed through my seaweed infested locks, relieved.

Mum tentatively paced the line where beach met water. Hesitant. Fearful. Superstitious as the pirates we ran aground. Rhea supported her in a half embrace. The brash sailor set aside her roughness for the moment, too focused on her mother to do otherwise.

"Declan? You're...alive? And a merrow at that!" Dad crowed. Joyful tears streamed down his cheeks. He cupped my face in his hands, laughing. His callouses scraped my skin, warm and familiar as the sun himself. I leaned into the touch, more than a little off balance. Dad stood waist deep in the waters, taller than I could ever hope to be.

"Dec?" Mum's voice wavered. She waded into the sea. Her eyes widened, full of more emotions than had names. Names in my language at least.

"Not what you remembered am I?"

Mum shook her head. Beneath the calm waves, Chika smothered a giggle. Her bubbles mingled with the surf around my mother. Rhea eyed the submerged sea-maiden with suspicion. She manoeuvred Mum around the glowing merrow and sighed.

A purple dorsal fin split the waves to our left. Valora rose demurely from the surf, her mauve-mottled skin shining violet in the starlight.

"Everyone is ashore." She turned her stern eyes upon my father and bowed her head. "You will find a small fishing village farther inland. Proceed as you see fit from there."

Dad nodded to her.

"Thank you," he said, offering a shallow bow. "And thank you for saving my son."

"Thank Chika." Valora dove into deeper water, unwilling to wait for a response.

"She's a terse one, ain't she?" Rhea snorted.

I shrugged. "At times."

Rhea hmphed and stretched, yawning loud enough to wake a slumbering ogre. The noise drew stares, as it always did, from merrow and human alike. Same old Rhea. Not even an abduction by pirates could rattle her habits.

"Well, I'm ready to find that village. Hope they have a nice inn that lets castaways stay for free or at least some decent grass to lay on. This way, Mum."

My thunderstruck mother followed Rhea out of the

water. She sat glumly on the rocks and stared into the middle-distance. Dad jogged out of the sea to join her. He rested a timeworn hand on his beloved's shoulder, his smile softening. Rhea paused with her toes barely in the surf.

"Aren't you coming?" she asked. I hesitated. After giving myself several long moments to consider my transformed body, I shook my head. A somber silence stretched the air.

"I'm going to do what our family has done for generations: protect the four seas. Only I am going to protect them from within rather than without."

Rhea's gaze found the waters. Her chest deflated as she masked a sigh.

"So…this is goodbye," she said. Not a question. A fact. One that clearly displeased her.

"Not quite." I rose out of the water, managing to balance on my fins. The sea steadied me. I caught Rhea in my finned arms and squeezed before she could protest. "I'll see you again, Sunray. I promise."

"Don't get lost, Dec. You owe us that much." Rhea shoved me away, grinning tearfully. A tenuous blush spread o'er my face. Hopefully, my sense of direction would improve over time. Meanwhile, I would heed Rhea's advice. Don't get lost. How hard could that be?

I dashed backward into the surf, letting the current take hold of me. The undertow hauled me into the depths. A new world awaited, as did Chika. Both promised adventures galore.

Epilogue

So it was that as clarity follows hindsight and moon-light follows sun, adventure followed incident and journeys were begun.

The tales and ballads of Zander were never-ending. They played on in an eternal cycle of reminiscence and wonder. Therefore, if one person remembered so much as a passing phrase, the story it stemmed from lived on until its every word faded beyond the scarcest recollection.

For the world of Zander was a double-edged sword, pervaded by light and darkness alike. One of blindness, sight, and Spectral Gaze. A land where Verve abounded and where adventure thrived. Then again, many worlds could be described that way. Even yours.

And just as with your world, the story is far from over.

About the Author

Winter Grace is the pen name I have assumed for your convenience and mine. I am an honest soul, but a great deal less blunt in person. Fellow humans see me as a petite little fifteen-year-old when in actuality I am a legal adult with a mental age I cannot hope to pinpoint. I adore tea, coffee, hot chocolate, books, music, music boxes, poetry, antiquities, and all sorts of things I do not have the patience to mention. I work when I must, sleep when I can, and love all my dear ones to the moon and back. As for my writing, I have done so for longer than I rightly know and hope to continue my literary journey for many years to come.

—Winter Grace

About the Illustrator

M. Adelle Laporte is a budding freelance artist and digital illustrator from the lower James Bay region. At 11 years old, she discovered her talent when she first started doodling on her grandmother's old chalkboard. Times have changed, but art remains a marvellous constant. Adelle has explored various styles and mediums, developing her skills thanks to many guiding hands (including Julia Martins, Lisa Mistiuk, Deb Hamby, and Gary Varvel). In 2022, she graduated from The Masters Guild with a certificate in entrepreneurial leadership and art, and she now works at a First Nations elementary school to finance her way through a communications degree.

Teacher by day and a student by night, Adelle takes every opportunity in between to indulge in freelance work. She has produced a vibrant, whimsical array of fine art portraits and digital storybook illustrations. As her clientele grows, Adelle hopes to use her talent and experience in team-based projects to build the beautiful worlds of today's new storytellers.